DRUMTHWACKET
AND OTHER ODDITIES
I HOPE YOU ENJOY

DRUMTHWACKET AND OTHER ODDITIES I HOPE YOU ENJOY

72 TRIVIA QUIZZES

COMPILED BY:

JOE DALEY AND FRIENDS

Table of Contents

FORWORD

First, please let me explain how this collection came about. I did not sit down with the idea of typing up a bunch of trivia match quizzes and compiling a book. Several friends had been meeting at our favorite watering hole for many years on Friday evenings. For a short period of time a few years ago the television program "Who Wants to be a Millionaire" would be on just before I could arrive. My friends would watch the show and when I arrived they would try to remember a few that they thought I might enjoy. Well, after the show left Friday nights we all seemed to miss it a bit so I decided to try to make up a little quiz from time to time. It did not take long before they became an integral part of our Friday nights and even gained a little popularity with the Saturday night crew as well. They were never the centerpiece of the evening as we were quite capable of amusing ourselves with a variety of other distractions but they did become popular enough that over the period of a few years I had accumulated well over one hundred. But all good things must come to an end, in Dec. 2003 our saloon closed its doors. For thirty years it had been just a small cocktail lounge in the center of a motel, restaurant and banquet facility. The regulars ranged from a young man not old enough to imbibe for the first several times he came in to a few that had already collected more from Social Security than they had ever paid in. The bar staff included both guys and girls one just 21 years old when he started to one part timer, yours truly, born when Harry Truman occupied the White House, all of whom could hold a reasonably intelligent conversation on a wide range of topics. The restaurant/banquet staff ranged from teenaged bus folks to those of us who were too old to disco. There were several instances of a second generation of the same family working there and the owners had the third generation tending the family business as their college schedules would allow. All in all it was a wonderful place to spend a little time, some off color language could be heard but problems were minor and rare. There were great friendships formed, a few marriages and divorces, births, illnesses and deaths, bad habits formed, good news proclaimed; the full range of life ensconced in our little corner of the world. I miss our little club house so as a paean to its existence I have compiled our little Friday evening pastimes into book form. I hope you enjoy them as much as we did.

ACKNOWLDGEMENTS

Of that corps of people that enjoyed the exercise enough to make me keep coming up with ideas I have to thank a few specifically. LeeAnn and Paul looked forward to the weekly trivia and inspired me to keep going more than anyone else, Debbie and Ed rarely missed a go at them and Joe Saviano was game for any subject but especially enjoyed the ones that required singing to solve. Although they were never part of the Friday night events, the girls, my Aunt Peggy, Aunt Mary and Mom always got a copy and between them could solve almost any test they attempted. I hope Aunts Peggy and Mary like this collection but Mother has gone to the land where all answers are known, I do miss her. Brother Bill tried his hand at several but more importantly helped me put this all together, without his help I would have never finished this project. There were many others, Karen Falbo and Patti Chapman and Lisa Mahoney, who types much better than I do, to name a few but I extend my heartfelt thanks to all who enjoyed them, helped think of a category, compile, type or edit this book. Thanks all, you're great.

INSTRUCTIONS

All you have to do is match something in column A (the numbered one) with something in column B (the lettered one). In most cases there are 26 items to match, none of which should be used twice. Most are simple, in the country capitol quiz you would match Ireland in column A to Dublin in column B. others are a bit more difficult. In the Working Vocabulary you will see that both a chef and a butcher may use a cleaver however there is another item mentioned that technically one trained only as a butcher is not entitled to use. I have tried to include a variety of categories to keep it interesting and fun. Some things, the name or existence of a sports stadium for instance, may have changed since the quiz was written, still you should be able to remember most. Solving some may require a dictionary, a textbook, a memory from long ago or just singing along till the pieces fall into place. Whatever it takes I hope you enjoy them. If you find a mistake or two please feel free to let me know. Thanks.

ALPHABET SOUP

1.	CHARLES, PRINCE OF WALES	A.	SPEBSQSA
2.	YOUR CAR CLUB	B.	NLRB
3.	FEDERAL TAX AGENCY	C.	PTA
4.	THE SHOOTING SPORTS	D.	HRH
5.	BROADCASTING LICENSES	E.	AKC
6.	PLANE CRASHES	F.	NRA
7.	JOB SAFETY	G.	ESQ
8.	CROOKED STOCKBROKERS	H.	ILGWU
9.	PARCEL POST	I.	FCC
10.	DEADLY DISEASES	J.	WHO
11.	THE NATIONAL BUDGET	K.	NASCAR
12.	A KIDNAPPING	L.	USPS
13.	AUTO RACING	M.	IRS
14.	A DOG'S PEDIGREE	N.	OSHA
15.	QUALITY OF MEAT	O.	DDS
16.	PRESCRIPTION MEDICATION	P.	NTSB
17.	FOLLOWS A LAWYERS NAME	Q.	DOT
18.	LET'S FORM A UNION	R.	AAA
19.	INSPECTS BIG RIGS	S.	BPOE
20.	SINGING 4 PART HARMONY	T.	SEC
21.	A UNION SEAMSTRESS	U.	OMB
22.	THE MORMONS	V.	FBI
23.	ROOT CANAL DR.	W.	USDA
24.	A SOCIAL SERVICE CLUB	X.	FDA
25.	A SCHOOL ORGANIZATION	Y.	CDC
26.	SHOTS BEFORE YOU TRAVEL	Z.	LDS

ANIMALS ETC.

1.	MANX	A.	AN ASIAN RODENT
2.	CLYDESDALE	B.	A DOMESTIC DOG (USED BY THE BRITISH)
3.	CAIMAN	C.	A KIND OF FALCON
4.	HEIFER	D.	NORTH AMERICAN RABBIT
5.	KODIAK	E.	A TYPE OF REINDEER
6.	HAMMERHEAD	F.	A WATER RODENT
7.	PEREGRINE	G.	A TYPE OF RATTLESNAKE
8.	SNOWSHOE	H.	A TYPE OF JELLYFISH
9.	ANGORA	I.	A TYPE OF TIGER
10.	MUTTON	J.	A VERY LARGE BEAR
11.	DUCKBILL	K.	A TYPE OF PENGUIN
12.	BACTRIAN	L.	A COW THAT NEVER CALVED
13.	WALLABY	M.	A TYPE OF SHARK
14.	SIDEWINDER	N.	A POISONOUS SPIDER
15.	NUTRIA	O.	A BABY SWAN
16.	VICUNA	P.	LIKE A SMALL KANGAROO
17.	DINGO	Q.	A PLATYPPUS
18.	JERABOA	R.	NICKNAME FOR A SKUNK
19.	MAN O' WAR	S.	OBTAINED FROM SHEEP
20.	WAPITI	T.	FINE HAIRED GOAT
21.	BENGAL	U.	LIKE A SMALL ALLIGATOR
22.	ALSATIAN	V.	AUSTRALIAN WILD DOG
23.	POLECAT	W.	A TAILLESS CAT
24.	EMPEROR	X.	TWO HUMPED CAMEL
25.	CYGNET	Y.	DRAFT HORSE
26.	BROWN RECLUSE	Z.	A SMALL LLAMA

ANIMAL WORDS

1.	ARACHNID	A.	CAT LIKE
2.	SERPENTINE	B.	BEAR LIKE
3.	TERRAPIN	C.	A GAME FISH
4.	WAPITI	D.	A MALE DUCK
5.	URSINE	E.	SPIDER
6.	MONARCH	F.	LIKE A KANGAROO
7.	QUAHOG	G.	A FLYING DINOSAUR
8.	PORCINE	H.	A POISONOUS LIZARD
9.	CASSOWARY	I.	A NOISY INSECT
10.	WILDEBEEST	J.	SNAKELIKE
11.	GANDER	K.	A BUTTERFLY TYPE
12.	CANINE	L.	A TURTLE TYPE
13.	KATYDID	M.	A LARGE SHRIMP
14.	WALLABY	N.	A MALE BEE
15.	PORTUGUESE MAN O' WAR	O.	AN OX FROM TIBET
16.	YAK	P.	COW LIKE
17.	BALEEN	Q.	A TYPE OF LLAMA
18.	FELINE	R.	PIG LIKE
19.	MUSKELLUNGE	S.	A GNU
20.	GILA MONSTER	T.	TYPE OF JELLYFISH
21.	DRONE	U.	A MALE GOOSE
22.	PRAWN	V.	A TYPE OF CLAM
23.	BOVINE	W.	DOG LIKE
24.	DRAKE	X.	A LARGE BIRD
25.	PTERODACTYL	Y.	A TYPE OF WHALE
26.	ALPACA	Z.	A REINDEER

ANIMALS IN FACT & FICTION

1.	TRIGGER	A.	OUR GANG
2.	CHECKERS	B.	THE JETSONS
3.	OLD BO	C.	PETE STERLING
4.	FRED	D.	AULD JACK
5.	ASTRO	E.	THE LONE RANGER
6.	LITTLE BLACKIE	F.	THE THIN MAN
7.	LASSIE	G.	F.D.R.
8.	BUTTERMILK	H.	TEDDY
9.	EDDIE	I.	GREY BEAVER
10.	SOCKS	J.	SHAGGY
11.	CUFF & LINK	K.	ROOSTER COGBURN
12.	FALA	L.	RUSTY
13.	SILVER	M.	ALEXANDER THE GREAT
14.	BOBBY (GREYFRIERS)	N.	MARTIN CRANE
15.	ASTA	O.	RICHARD M. NIXON
16.	MILLIE	P.	WILBUR POST
17.	BUCEPHALUS	Q.	DALE EVANS
18.	SCOOBY DO	R.	JOHN STEINBECK
19.	PETEY (PETE THE PUP)	S.	TIMMY
20.	WHITE FANG	T.	ROBERT E. LEE
21.	MR. ED	U.	BILL CLINTON
22.	RIN TIN TIN	V.	BARETTA
23.	RIKKI TIKKI TAVI	W.	ROY ROGERS
24.	CHARLEY	X.	BARBARA BUSH
25.	TRAVELLER	Y.	ROCKY BALBOA
26.	FRANCIS THE TALKING MULE	Z.	MATTI ROSS (TRUE GRIT)

WHEN I GROW UP I WANT TO BE A

1.	ANTLING	A.	CLAM
2.	KIT	B.	SHEEP
3.	PUSSY	C.	BUFFALO
4.	NESTLING	D.	RABBIT
5.	SPIKE BULL	E.	ANT
6.	SMOLTS	F.	CHICKEN
7.	KID	G.	DEER
8.	TADPOLE	H.	SEAL
9.	SHOAT	I.	GOAT
10.	BUNNY	J.	BEAR
11.	WHELP	K.	KANGAROO
12.	POULT	L.	PIGEON
13.	ELVER	M.	OWL
14.	FOAL	N.	CAT
15.	SQUAB	O.	FROG
16.	SPAWN	P.	SQUIRREL
17.	JOEY	Q.	BIRD (FALCON)
18.	HOWLET	R.	GOOSE
19.	LITTLENECK	S.	SALMON
20.	CYGNET	T.	FISH (TROUT)
21.	LAMB	U.	PIG
22.	BACHELOR	V.	DOG
23.	CUB	W.	FOX
24.	DRAY	X.	HORSE
25.	FAWN	Y.	SWAN
26.	GOSLING	Z.	EEL

MAKES AND MODELS

1.	AMIGO	A.	AMC
2.	APOLLO	B.	VOLKSWAGEN
3.	AURORA	C.	LAMBORGHINI
4.	CIMARRON	D.	HONDA
5.	COMANCHE	E.	RENAULT
6.	CORDOBA	F.	TOYOTA
7.	COSMOPOLITAN	G.	AUDI
8.	CRESSIDA	H.	CHEVROLET
9.	DAYTONA SPYDER	I.	OLDSMOBILE
10.	DELSOL	J.	JEEP
11.	DIPLOMAT	K.	ISUZU
12.	ESPADA	L.	MAZDA
13.	FAIRLANE	M.	PONTIAC
14.	FOX	N.	MERCURY
15.	FUEGO	O.	MITSUBISHI
16.	JAVELIN	P.	NISSAN
17.	LEMANS	Q.	FERRARI
18.	MILLENIA	R.	HYUNDAI
19.	MONZA	S.	FORD
20.	PULSAR	T.	DODGE
21.	SCIROCCO	U.	CADILLAC
22.	SIERRA	V.	LINCOLN
23.	STARION	W.	PLYMOUTH
24.	TIBURON	X.	CHRYSLER
25.	VOLARE	Y.	BUICK
26.	ZEPHER	Z.	GMC TRUCK

Thanks to Paul and Caesar

FROM THE BIBLE

1.	NOAH	A.	SUCCESSOR TO ELIJAH
2.	JOB	B.	FIRST KING OF ISRAEL
3.	LOT	C.	KNOWN FOR HIS WISDOM
4.	DELILAH	D.	DANCED FOR JOHN'S HEAD
5.	SOLOMON	E.	OLDER BROTHER OF ABEL
6.	MELCHIOR	F.	BUILT THE ARK
7.	AARON	G.	RAISED FROM THE DEAD
8.	DAVID	H.	HIS WIFE TURNED TO SALT
9.	GABRIEL	I.	LIVED TO AGE 969
10.	JOSHUA	J.	KNOWN FOR GREAT PATIENCE
11.	DANIEL	K.	MOTHER OF JOHN THE BAPTIST
12.	ISSAC	L.	OLDER BROTHER OF MOSES
13.	ABEDNEGO	M.	GREAT GRANDMOTHER OF DAVID
14.	CAIN	N.	AN EARLY JUDAIC PRIEST
15.	ELIZABETH	O.	SWALLOWED BY A WHALE
16.	CAIAPHAS	P.	KNOWS GASPAR & BALTHASAR
17.	RUTH	Q.	BECAME QUEEN OF PERSIA
18.	METHUSELAH	R.	FACED LIONS IN THEIR DENS
19.	ELISHA	S.	FULL OF DOUBT
20.	SAUL	T.	TEMPTED SAMPSON
21.	SALOME	U.	SON OF ABRAHAM
22.	LAZARUS	V.	FOUGHT AT JERICO
23.	ESTHER	W.	FRIENDS, SHADRACH & MESHACH
24.	JONAH	X.	CHARGED JESUS WITH BLASPHEMY
25.	THOMAS	Y.	AN ARCHANGEL
26.	MELCHISEDECH	Z.	SLEW THE GIANT

PATRON SAINTS

1.	BATTLE	A.	STAINISLAUS
2.	BREWERS	B.	FRANCIS OF ASSISI
3.	CARPENTERS	C.	JOAN OF ARC
4.	CATHOLIC CHARITIES	D.	THOMAS MOORE
5.	CEMETERY KEEPERS	E.	ARCHANGEL MICHAEL
6.	MOTHERS	F.	COSMOS AND DAMIEN
7.	CIVIL SERVANTS.	G.	DISMAS
8.	COLLEGES	H.	VALENTINE
9.	DANCERS	I.	WENCESLAUS
10.	ENGLAND	J.	PATRICK
11.	FISHERMAN	K.	CHARLES BORROMEO
12.	FLORISTS	L.	JUDE
13.	FRANCE	M.	VINCENT DE PAUL
14.	IRELAND	N.	ANNE
15.	ITALY	O.	VITUS
16.	JOURNEYS	P.	MARK
17.	LOST CAUSES	Q.	GEORGE
18.	LOVERS	R.	BASIL THE GREAT
19.	PHARMACISTS	S.	THOMAS AQUINAS
20.	POLAND	T.	BLAISE
21.	RUSSIA	U.	ROSE OF LIMA
22.	SCOTLAND	V.	PETER
23.	SEMINARIANS	W.	JOSEPH OF ARIMATHEA
24.	THIEVES (GOOD ONES?)	X.	ANDREW
25.	THROAT AILMENTS	Y.	JOSEPH
26.	VENICE	Z.	CHRISTOPHER

A VERY CATHOLIC VOCABULARY

1.	ABSOLUTION	A.	BISHOPS HAT
2.	ALB	B.	WORD SPOKEN OR SUNG IN PRAISE
3.	BETHROTHAL	C.	WHERE CHRIST WAS CRUCIFIED
4.	BEATIFIED	D.	A TRUTH OF FAITH OR MORALS
5.	CANA	E.	REMISSION OF SINS
6.	CASSOCK	F.	SERMON AFTER THE GOSPEL
7.	EX CATHEDRA	G.	LAST RITES OF THE CHURCH
8.	DOGMA	H.	A PRAYER TO OUR LADY
9.	ENCYCLICAL	I.	OUR FATHER
10.	EXORCISM	J.	I CONFESS TO GOD
11.	EXTREME UNCTION	K.	A WHITE LINEN VESTMENT
12.	GETHSEMANI	L.	BENDING 1 KNEE TO THE GROUND
13.	GOLGOTHA	M.	THE PEACE OF THE LORD
14.	HOMILY	N.	GREEK FOR LORD HAVE MERCY
15.	HOSANNA	O.	PRIESTS 33 BUTTON VESTMENT
16.	INQUISITION	P.	AND WITH THY SPIRIT
17.	GENUFLEXION	Q.	LET US PRAY
18.	KYRIE ELEISON	R.	SITE OF CHRISTS FIRST MIRACLE
19.	MAGNIFICAT	S.	THE LORD BE WITH YOU
20.	MITRE	T.	POPES LETTER ABOUT FAITH
21.	ET CUM SPIRITU TUO	U.	A PROMISE OF MARRIAGE
22.	PATER NOSTER	V.	GARDEN OF CHRISTS ARREST
23.	CONFIETOR DEO	W.	STEP TOWARD SAINTHOOD
24.	DOMINUS VOBISCUM	X.	FROM THE BISHOPS CHAIR
25.	OREMUS	Y.	RITUAL TO DRIVE OUT DEMONS
26.	PAX DOMINI	Z.	COURT INVESTIGATING HERESY

A VERY JEWISH VOCABULARY

WITH A LITTLE YIDDISH THROWN IN

1.	BABUSHKA	A.	TRADITIONAL PRAYER OF MOURNING
2.	BAT/BAR MITZVA	B.	OH NO (PHRASE OF GRIEF OR PAIN)
3.	BUBBY	C.	A/TO SNACK
4.	BUPKES	D.	A KERCHIEF AS A HEADCOVERING
5.	CHUTZPAH	E.	PEACE (USED AS A GREETING)
6.	DREIDEL	F.	THE ISRAELI PARLIAMENT
7.	GELT	G.	THE HOLOCAUST
8.	HORA	H.	A CRAZY PERSON
9.	KADDISH	I.	A TOAST, MEANING "TO LIFE"
10.	KIBBUTZ	J.	SOMETHING WORTHLESS
11.	KLEZMER	K.	THE SABBATH DAY
12.	KNESSET	L.	A GIRL/BOY COMING OF AGE CERMONY
13.	LIKUD	M.	TO CARRY A LOAD
14.	L'CHAIM	N.	TOY TOP USED AT CHANUKAH
15.	MAZEL TOV	O.	A SKULL CAP
16.	MENSCH	P.	AN ISRAELI COLLECTIVE FARM
17.	MESHUGENE	Q.	NERVE OR GALL
18.	NOSH	R.	MUSICAL INST. MADE FROM A RAMS HORN
19.	OY VEY	S.	A STYLE OF MUSIC
20.	SCHLEP	T.	A GRANDMOTHER
21.	SEDER	U.	A FESTIVE CIRCLE DANCE
22.	SHABBAT	V.	A PHRASE OF CONGRATULATIONS
23.	SHALOM	W.	A GOOD GUY OR REAL MAN
24.	SHOAH	X.	MONEY (ESP. GIVEN AT CHANUKAH)
25.	SHOFAR	Y.	A CEREMONIAL MEAL
26.	YARMULKE	Z.	ISRAEL'S CONSERVATIVE PARTY

I'M SO HUNGRY I COULD EAT A HORSE

IF I KNEW WHICH OF THESE WAS A HORSE

1.	ESCARGOT	A.	RANCH STYLE EGGS
2.	COQ A VAN	B.	SOUR ROASTED BEEF
3.	COQUILLE ST JACQUES	C.	BEET SOUP
4.	L'OUEF	D.	FISH
5.	BORSCHT	E.	PICKELED OCTOPUS
6.	BANGERS & MASH	F.	VEAL SHANK (STEWED)
7.	LE GLAZE	G.	BRAISED RABBIT
8.	POLLOS CON ARROZ	H.	SPICY ITALIAN HAM
9.	GAZPACHO	I.	BREAST OF CHICKEN
10.	SPOTTED DICK	J.	CHICKEN IN WINE
11.	SAUERBRATEN	K.	EGG
12.	WIENER SCHNITZEL	L.	MACARONI & BEAN SOUP
13.	BASHED NEEPS	M.	SAUSAGES & MASHED POTATOS
14.	LE JAMBON	N.	SNAILS
15.	HUEVOS RANCHEROS	O.	DONUTS
16.	OSSO BUCCO*	P.	COLD VEGETABLE SOUP
17.	PAIN AU CITRON	Q.	BREADED VEAL CUTLET
18.	PASTA FAZOLLE**	R.	CABBAGE & MEAT MIX
19.	PROSCIUTTO	S.	CHICKEN WITH RICE
20.	OKTAPODI TOURSI	T.	MEATBALL SOUP
21.	HASENPFEFFER	U.	SWEET SUET PASTRY
22.	LE POISSON	V.	MASHED TURNIPS
23.	FASTNACHTS	W.	ICE CREAM
24.	PETTO DE POLLO	X.	HAM
25.	BUBBLE & SQUEEK	Y.	LEMON BREAD
26.	SOPA DE ALBONDIGUITAS	Z.	SCALLOPS/POTATOS /MUSH ROOMS/CHEESE

* LIT. CLAY POT   ** ALSO FAGIOLI

BEERS OF THE WORLD

1.	AUSTRALIA	A.	HEINEKEN
2.	AUSTRIA	B.	SAPPORO
3.	BAHAMAS	C.	MACCABEE
4.	BELGIUM	D.	SNECK LIFFER
5.	CANADA	E.	LA ROSSA BIRRA
6.	CZECH REPUBLIC	F.	RAFFLE'S EXPORT
7.	DENMARK	G.	ZYWIEC
8.	ENGLAND	H.	TENNENT'S
9.	GERMANY	I.	LABATT'S
10.	HOLLAND	J.	FOSTER'S
11.	IRELAND	K.	RED STRIPE
12.	ISRAEL	L.	CARIB LAGER
13.	ITALY	M.	BLACK TIGER
14.	JAMAICA	N.	STELLA ARTIOS
15.	JAPAN	O.	CUSQUENA
16.	MEXICO	P.	KALIK
17.	PERU	Q.	CARLSBERG
18.	PHILIPPINES	R.	BLACK BEARD
19.	POLAND	S.	EGGER LEICHT
20.	SCOTLAND	T.	OSMA SURETLE
21.	SINGAPORE	U.	HUE BEER
22.	THAILAND	V.	GUINNESS STOUT
23.	VIETNAM	W.	WHITBREAD TROPHY
24.	VIRGIN ISLANDS	X.	SAN MIGUEL
25.	WALES	Y.	DINKEL ACKER
26.	WEST INDIES	Z.	TECATE

COCKTAILS ANYONE?

1.	SCREWDRIVER	A.	SCOTCH, DRAMBUIE
2.	MARTINI	B.	VODKA, TOMATO JUICE, SPICES
3.	OLD FASHIONED	C.	BOURBON, MINT, WATER, SUGAR
4.	BLOODY MARY	D.	RUM, COKE, LIME
5.	STINGER	E.	RYE, SWEET VERMOUTH
6.	MANHATTAN	F.	GIN, SUGAR, LIME JUICE
7.	GIMLET	G.	GIN, DRY VERMOUTH
8.	SOMBRERO	H.	CHAMPAGNE, ORANGE JUICE
9.	MUD SLIDE	I.	TEQUILA, TRIPLE SEC, LIME JUICE
10.	ROB ROY	J.	GIN, SOUR MIX, CLUB SODA
11.	DAIQUIRI	K.	VODKA, PEACH SCHNAPPS, CRANBERRY
12.	MINT JULEP	L.	KAHULA, AMARETTO, CREAM
13.	SALTY DOG	M.	VODKA, ORANGE JUICE
14.	JACK ROSE	N.	GRAND MARINER, KAHULA, BAILEYS
15.	TOM COLLINS	O.	RUM, SOUR MIX, GRENADINE
16.	CUBA LIBRE	P.	VODKA, KAHULA, BAILEY'S
17.	GODFATHER	Q.	VODKA, KAHULA
18.	MARGARITA	R.	KAHULA, CREAM
19.	FUZZY NAVAL	S.	VODKA, GRAPEFRUIT JUICE, SALT
20.	MIMOSA	T.	RYE, MUDDLED FRUIT, BITTERS, SUGAR
21.	RUSTY NAIL	U.	BRANDY, CREME DE MENTHE
22.	BLACK RUSSIAN	V.	SCOTCH, AMARETTO
23.	TOASTED ALMOND	W.	RUM, SUGAR, SOUR MIX
24.	BACARDI COCKTAIL	X.	APPLE JACK, SOUR MIX, GRENADINE
25.	B-52'S	Y.	PEACH SCHNAPPS, ORANGE JUICE
26.	WOO WOO	Z.	SCOTCH, SWEET VERMOUTH

"B" ON THE MAP

1.	BADEN-BADEN	A.	FRANCE
2.	BAHIA DE CUCHINOS	B.	SLOVAKIA
3.	BAGHDAD	C.	SPAIN
4.	BANFF	D.	NORWAY
5.	BARCELONA	E.	BRAZIL
6.	BARRANQUILLA	F.	INDIA
7.	BATH	G.	LEBANON
8.	BATON ROUGE	H.	CANADA
9.	BEIJING	I.	GERMANY
10.	BEIRUT	J.	YUGOSLAVIA
11.	BELFAST	K.	RUMANIA
12.	BELGRADE	L.	POLAND
13.	BERGEN	M.	AUSTRALIA
14.	BERN	N.	ENGLAND
15.	BIALYSTOK	O.	BELGIUM
16.	BIEN HOA	P.	REPUBLIC OF THE CONGO
17.	BOMBAY	Q.	U.S.A.
18.	BOLOGNA	R.	HUNGARY
19.	BORDEAUX	S.	IRAQ
20.	BRASILIA	T.	CHINA
21.	BRATISLAVA	U.	SWITZERLAND
22.	BRAZZAVILLE	V.	CUBA
23.	BRISBANE	W.	COLUMBIA
24.	BRUSSELS	X.	VIETNAM
25.	BUCHAREST	Y.	N. IRELAND
26.	BUDAPEST	Z.	ITALY

"M" ON THE MAP

1.	MADRAS	A.	KENYA
2.	MADRID	B.	URUGUAY
3.	MALMO	C.	ENGLAND
4.	MANAGUA	D.	CANADA
5.	MANCHESTER	E.	PHILIPPINES
6.	MANDALAY	F.	ITALY
7.	MANILA	G.	MEXICO
8.	MARACAIBO	H.	NICARAGUA
9.	MARRAKECH	I.	GERMANY
10.	MAZATLAN	J.	COLUMBIA
11.	MECCA	K.	RUSSIA
12.	MEDELLIN	L.	U.S.A.
13.	MEDICINE HAT	M.	JAPAN
14.	MELBOURNE	N.	OMAN
15.	MESSINA	O.	MOROCCO
16.	MINSK	P.	LIBERIA
17.	MITO	Q.	VENEZUELA
18.	MOGADISHU	R.	SWEDEN
19.	MOMBASA	S.	BURMA (MYANMAR)
20.	MONROVIA	T.	SPAIN
21.	MONTEVIDEO	U.	SAUDI ARABIA
22.	MONTE CARLO	V.	BELARUS
23.	MONTPELIER	W.	AUSTRALIA
24.	MUNICH	X.	MONACO
25.	MURMANSK	Y.	SOMALIA
26.	MUSCAT	Z.	INDIA

"S" ON THE MAP

1.	SAARBRUCKEN	A.	CHINA
2.	SAIGON	B.	RHODESIA
3.	SAINT CROIX	C.	ENGLAND
4.	SALERNO	D.	SCOTLAND
5.	SALISBURY	E.	CANADA
6.	SALONIKA	F.	JAPAN
7.	SALZBURG	G.	U.S.A.
8.	SAN JUAN	H.	GERMANY
9.	SAN LUIS OBISPO	I.	BULGARIA
10.	SANTIAGO	J.	ITALY
11.	SAO PAULO	K.	FIJI
12.	SAPPORO	L.	PUERTO RICO
13.	SARAJEVO	M.	VIETNAM
14.	SASKATOON	N.	NORWAY
15.	SEOUL	O.	WALES
16.	SEVASTOPOL	P.	GREECE
17.	SEVILLE	Q.	SWEDEN
18.	SHANGHAI	R.	EGYPT
19.	SHETLAND ISLANDS	S.	AUSTRIA
20.	SOFIA	T.	BRAZIL
21.	SPITSBERGEN	U.	SOUTH KOREA
22.	STAFFORDSHIRE	V.	CHILE
23.	STOCKHOLM	W.	US VIRGIN ISLANDS
24.	SUEZ	X.	BOSNIA
25.	SUVA	Y.	UKRAINE
26.	SWANSEA	Z.	SPAIN

RIVERS & CITIES

1. DELAWARE
2. MISSISSIPPI
3. WHITE
4. OHIO
5. PENOBSCOT
6. POTOMAC
7. CHARLES
8. MERRIMACK
9. ARKANSAS
10. COLUMBIA
11. NILE
12. SEINE
13. SCHUYLKILL
14. CUMBERLAND
15. SOUTH CANADIAN
16. DANUBE
17. MONONGAHELA
18. RIO GRANDE
19. LEHIGH
20. JAMES
21. THAMES
22. NIAGARA
23. SUSQUEHANNA
24. NORTH PLATTE
25. TIBER
26. COLORADO

A. CASPER WY
B. EL PASO TX
C. PHILADELPHIA, PA
D. ROME, ITALY
E. ALLENTOWN, PA
F. RICHMOND, VA
G. OKLAHOMA CITY, OK
H. BUFFALO, NY
I. VIENNA, AUSTRIA
J. INDIANAPOLIS, IN
K. WASHINGTON, DC
L. LONDON, ENGLAND
M. LOUISVILLE, KY
N. TULSA, OK
O. LAKE HAVASU CITY, AZ
P. MINNEAPOLIS, MN
Q. HARRISBURG, PA
R. READING, PA
S. BANGOR, ME
T. PORTLAND, OR
U. NASHVILLE, TN
V. DUQUESNE, PA
W. MANCHESTER, NH
X. PARIS, FRANCE
Y. BOSTON, MA
Z. CAIRO, EGYPT

WHERE ARE YOU FROM

1.	THE BIG APPLE	A.	ST AUGUSTINE, FL
2.	MILE HIGH CITY	B.	NEW ORLEANS, LA
3.	WORLDS MOST FAMOUS BEACH	C.	ATLANTA, GA
4.	CITY OF FIVE SEASONS	D.	BOSTON, MA
5.	CITY OF LAKES	E.	BOISE, ID
6.	GATEWAY TO THE WEST	F.	NEW YORK, NY
7.	THE MOTOR CITY	G.	SAN FRANCISCO, CA
8.	THE MUSIC CITY	H.	LOUISVILLE, KY
9.	CITY OF BROTHERLY LOVE	I.	MINNEAPOLIS, MN
10.	THE BIG PEACH	J.	CINCINNATI, OH
11.	CHARM CITY	K.	DAYTONA BEACH, FL
12.	SOUL OF THE SOUTHWEST	L.	PHILADELPHIA, PA
13.	SHOW CAPITOL OF THE WORLD	M.	INDIANAPOLIS, IN
14.	THE WINDY CITY	N.	LOS ANGELES, CA
15.	THE QUEEN CITY	O.	DENVER, CO
16.	DERBYTOWN	P.	LAS VEGAS, NV
17.	THE EMERALD CITY	Q.	NASHVILLE, TN
18.	THE CRESENT CITY	R.	RENO, NV
19.	THE CITY BY THE BAY	S.	ST LOUIS, MO
20.	THE CIRCLE CITY	T.	PHOENIX, AZ
21.	THE CITY OF ANGELS	U.	BALTIMORE, MD
22.	THE ANCIENT CITY	V.	TAOS, NM
23.	BEANTOWN	W.	CEDAR RAPIDS, IA
24.	VALLEY OF THE SUN	X.	SEATTLE, WA
25.	THE CITY OF TREES	Y.	DETROIT, MI
26.	THE BIGGEST LITTLE CITY IN THE WORLD	Z.	CHICAGO, IL

U.S. STATE NICKNAMES

1.	ALASKA	A.	THE KEYSTONE STATE
2.	ARKANSAS	B.	THE SUNFLOWER STATE
3.	CALIFORNIA	C.	LAND OF ENCHANTMENT
4.	COLORADO	D.	THE LAST FRONTIER
5.	CONNECTICUT	E.	THE BAY STATE
6.	DELAWARE	F.	THE HAWKEYE STATE
7.	GEORGIA	G.	THE GARDEN STATE
8.	IDAHO	H.	THE GOLDEN STATE
9.	IOWA	I.	THE SILVER STATE
10.	KANSAS	J.	THE PINE TREE STATE
11.	LOUISIANA	K.	THE NORTH STAR STATE
12.	MAINE	L.	THE EQUALITY STATE (COWBOY)
13.	MARYLAND	M.	THE TREASURE STATE
14.	MASSACHUSETTS	N.	THE CONSTITUTION STATE
15.	MINNESOTA	O.	THE GRANITE STATE
16.	MISSISSIPPI	P.	THE DIAMOND STATE
17.	MONTANA	Q.	THE NATURAL STATE
18.	NEVADA	R.	THE MAGNOLIA STATE
19.	NEW HAMPSHIRE	S.	THE OLD DOMINION STATE
20.	NEW JERSEY	T.	THE BEAVER STATE
21.	NEW MEXICO	U.	THE CENTENIAL STATE
22.	OREGON	V.	THE BEHIVE STATE
23.	PENNSYLVANIA	W.	THE GEM STATE
24.	UTAH	X.	THE PELICAN STATE
25.	VIRGINIA	Y.	THE PEACH STATE
26.	WYOMING	Z.	THE OLD LINE STATE

STATE CAPITOLS

1.	ALABAMA	A.	JACKSON
2.	ARKANSAS	B.	AUGUSTA
3.	IDAHO	C.	ST. PAUL
4.	ILLINOIS	D.	SALEM
5.	IOWA	E.	HELENA
6.	KANSAS	F.	JEFFESON CITY
7.	KENTUCKY	G.	LINCOLN
8.	LOUISIANA	H.	MADISON
9.	MAINE	I.	CONCORD
10.	MARYLAND	J.	PIERRE
11.	MICHIGAN	K.	MONTGOMERY
12.	MINNESOTA	L.	BATON ROUGE
13.	MISSISSIPPI	M.	BISMARCK
14.	MISSOURI	N.	OLYMPIA
15.	MONTANA	O.	BOISE
16.	NEBRASKA	P.	SPRINGFIELD
17.	NEVADA	Q.	LANSING
18.	NEW HAMPSHIRE	R.	COLUMBIA
19.	NORTH DAKOTA	S.	TOPEKA
20.	OREGON	T.	MONTPELIER
21.	SOUTH CAROLINA	U.	DES MOINES
22.	SOUTH DAKOTA	V.	CHARLESTON
23.	VERMONT	W.	FRANKFORT
24.	WASHINGTON	X.	LITTLE ROCK
25.	WEST VIRGINIA	Y.	ANNAPOLIS
26.	WISCONSIN	Z.	CARSON CITY

NATIONAL PARKS BY STATE

1.	SARATOGA NAT'L HISTORICAL PARK	A.	GEORGIA
2.	EVERGLADES NAT'L PARK	B.	SOUTH CAROLINA
3.	ACADIA NATIONAL PARK	C.	NEW MEXICO
4.	VICKSBURG NATIONAL PARK	D.	UTAH
5.	ZION NATIONAL PARK	E.	MARYLAND
6.	HARPER'S FERRY NAT'L HISTORY PARK	F.	SOUTH DAKOTA
7.	YELLOWSTONE NATIONAL PARK	G.	MISSISSIPPI
8.	BADLANDS NAT'L PARK	H.	NEW YORK
9.	PETRIFIED FOREST NAT'L PARK	I.	WASHINGTON
10.	ANDERSONVILLE NAT'L HIST SITE	J.	ARIZONA
11.	JEAN LAFITE NAT'L PARK	K.	NEVADA
12.	VALLEY FORGE NAT'L HIST. PARK	L.	CALIFORNIA
13.	NEZ PERCE NAT'L HIST. PARK	M.	ALASKA
14.	MOUNT RAINIER NAT'L PARK	N.	FLORIDA
15.	FORT SUMTER NAT'L MONUMENT	O.	VIRGINIA
16.	ANTIETAM NAT'L CEMETERY	P.	WYOMING
17.	CRATER LAKE NAT'L PARK	Q.	MAINE
18.	VOYAGEURS NAT'L PARK	R.	LOUISIANA
19.	CARLSBAD CAVERNS NAT'L PARK	S.	ARKANSAS
20.	BIG BEND NAT'L PARK	T.	KENTUCKY
21.	YOSEMITE NAT'L PARK	U.	IDAHO
22.	SHENANDOAH NAT'L PARK	V.	OREGON
23.	GREAT BASIN NAT'L PARK	W.	WEST VIRGINIA
24.	HOT SPRINGS NAT'L PARK	X.	TEXAS
25.	DENALI NAT'L PARK	Y.	PENNSYLVANIA
26.	MAMOTH CAVE NATIONAL PARK	Z.	MINNESOTA

TOURIST TRAPS

1.	THE LIBERTY BELL	A.	RAPID CITY, SD
2.	GRANTS TOMB	B.	LOUISVILLE, KY
3.	THE SPACE NEEDLE	C.	LAS VEGAS, NV
4.	THE GATEWAY ARCH	D.	PHILADELPHIA, PA
5.	"GRACE LAND"	E.	INDIANAPOLIS, IN
6.	THE PRESIDIO	F.	WASHINGTON, DC
7.	SEARS TOWER	G.	MEMPHIS, TN
8.	FANEUIL HALL	H.	SEATTLE, WA
9.	(HMS) QUEEN MARY	I.	ARLINGTON, VA
10.	PIKES PEAK	J.	ORLANDO, FL
11.	THE ALAMO	K.	NEW ORLEANS, LA
12.	HOOVER DAM	L.	HONOLULU, HI
13.	FORT SUMTER	M.	LAKE HAVASU CITY, AZ
14.	MT. RUSHMORE	N.	BOSTON, MA
15.	E. A. POES GRAVE	O.	ATLANTA, GA
16.	MAMMOTH CAVE	P.	NEW YORK, NY
17.	THE ROSE BOWL	Q.	SAN ANTONIO, TX
18.	THE LONDON BRIDGE	R.	ST LOUIS, MO
19.	"THE BRICKYARD"	S.	CHICAGO, IL
20.	USS ARIZONA MEMORIAL	T.	CHARLESTON, SC
21.	"FRENCH QUARTER"	U.	SAN FRANCISCO, CA
22.	CHURCHILL DOWNS	V.	BOWLING GREEN, KY
23.	THE TOMB OF THE UNKNOWN SOLIDER	W.	PASADENA, CA
24.	STONE MOUNTAIN	X.	LONG BEACH, CA
25.	THE SMITHSONIAN INST.	Y.	BALTIMORE, MD
26.	THE EXPERIMENTAL PROTOTYPE COMMUNITY OF TOMORROW	Z.	COLORADO SPRINGS, CO

I FLEW TO CHICAGO HOW DID

MY BAGS GET TO PARIS?

1.	LAX	A.	KANSAS CITY, MO
2.	LHR	B.	TOKYO, JAPAN
3.	SLC	C.	SAN FRANCISCO, CA
4.	SNN	D.	WASHINGTON (NATIONAL)
5.	ORY	E.	ORLANDO, FL
6.	ABQ	F.	SAN JOSE, CA
7.	BWI	G.	HONOLULU, HI
8.	SJU	H.	LOS ANGELES INTL
9.	MCO	I.	ROME, ITALY
10.	ORD	J.	SHANNON, IRELAND
11.	DFW	K.	MINNEAPOLIS, MN
12.	EWR	L.	LONDON'S HEATHROW
13.	MKC	M.	LAS VEGAS, NV
14.	DCA	N.	BALTIMORE, MD
15.	NRT	O.	ALBUQUERQUE, NM
16.	IAH	P.	NEWARK, NJ
17.	PHX	Q.	NEW YORK, NY (LA GUARDIA)
18.	HNL	R.	PARIS, FRANCE
19.	ABE	S.	CHICAGO (O'HARE)
20.	LAS	T.	SALT LAKE CITY, UT
21.	FCO	U.	HONG KONG
22.	SFO	V.	DALLAS, TX
23.	MSP	W.	PHOENIX, AZ
24.	LGA	X.	SAN JUAN, PUERTO RICO
25.	HKG	Y.	HOUSTON, TX
26.	SJC	Z.	ALLENTOWN, PA

MATCH THE CAPITOL CITY

TO IT'S COUNTRY

1.	IRELAND		A.	TRIPOLI
2.	EGYPT		B.	BANGKOK
3.	URUGUAY		C.	WARSAW
4.	CANADA		D.	MADRID
5.	POLAND		E.	BAGHDAD
6.	SPAIN		F.	STOCKHOLM
7.	PORTUGAL		G.	DUBLIN
8.	FINLAND		H.	TEHRAN
9.	SWEDEN		I.	OTTAWA
10.	WALES		J.	RABAT
11.	AUSTRALIA		K.	LIMA
12.	PHILIPPINES		L.	VIENNA
13.	COLUMBIA		M.	SEOUL
14.	IRAN		N.	CAIRO
15.	PERU		O.	CARDIFF
16.	CHILE		P.	NAIROBI
17.	LIBERIA		Q.	NEW DELHI
18.	IRAQ		R.	SANTIAGO
19.	LIBYA		S.	CANBERRA
20.	MOROCCO		T.	MONTEVIDEO
21.	THAILAND		U.	BRUSSELS
22.	KENYA		V.	MANILA
23.	SOUTH KOREA		W.	LISBON
24.	INDIA		X.	MONROVIA
25.	AUSTRIA		Y.	HELSINKI
26.	BELGIUM		Z.	BOGOTA

WORLD LEADERS

THEN AND NOW

1.	ARGENTINA	A.	ALBERTO FUJIMORI
2.	CANADA	B.	LECH WALESA
3.	CHINA	C.	ANWAR SADAT
4.	CUBA	D.	KIM IL SUNG
5.	EGYPT	E.	SADDAM HUSSEIN
6.	ENGLAND	F.	GOLDA MEIR
7.	FRANCE	G.	JUAN PERON
8.	INDIA	H.	FIDEL CASTRO
9.	IRAN	I.	IDI AMIN
10.	IRAQ	J.	VINCENTE FOX
11.	IRELAND	K.	FRANCISCO FRANCO
12.	ISRAEL	L.	PIERRE ELLIOT TRUDEAU
13.	ITALY	M.	BORIS YELTSIN
14.	JAPAN	N.	AYATOLLAH KHOMEINI
15.	NORTH KOREA	O.	WINSTON CHURCHILL
16.	LYBIA	P.	DWIGHT EISENHOWER
17.	MEXICO	Q.	EMPEROR HIROHITO
18.	PANAMA	R.	MUAMMAR AL-QADDAFI
19.	PERU	S.	NELSON MANDELA
20.	PHILIPPINES	T.	MAO TSE-TUNG
21.	POLAND	U.	CHARLES DE GAULLE
22.	RUSSIA	V.	EAMON DE VALERA
23.	SPAIN	W.	MANUEL NORIEGA
24.	SOUTH AFRICA	X.	BENITO MUSSOLINI
25.	UGANDA	Y.	CORAZON AQUINO
26.	UNITED STATES	Z.	INDIRA GANDHI

EUROPEAN TRAVELS

1.	OUI, MERCI BEACOUP	A.	100,000 WELCOMES
2.	PARLEZ-VOUS ANGLAIS.	B.	TRUTH
3.	SPRECHEN SIE DEUTSCH	C.	WELCOME
4.	AUF WIEDERSEHEN	D.	THANK YOU
5.	CEDE MIL FALTE	E.	BATHROOM
6.	NON CAPISCO	F.	ONE BEER, PLEASE
7.	BUON GIORNO	G.	DO YOU TAKE CREDIT CARDS?
8.	GOEDENACHT.	H.	TO YOUR HEALTH
9.	WAAR IS.	I.	GOOD MORNING
10.	VELKOMMEN	J.	DO YOU SPEAK ENGLISH?
11.	TAKK	K.	BUS
12.	QUARTO DE BANHO	L.	GOODBYE
13.	AUTOCARRO	M.	DO YOU SPEAK GERMAN
14.	PRAVDA	N.	UMBRELLA
15.	UNA CERVEZA, POR FAVOR	O.	GOOD NIGHT
16.	DONDE ESTA LOS SERVICIOS.	P.	CAR TRUNK
17.	SKAL	Q.	I DON'T UNDERSTAND
18.	KAN JAG BETALA MED KREDITKORT	R.	YES, THANK YOU VERY MUCH
19.	BROLLY	S.	WHERE IS THE MENS ROOM?
20.	BOOT	T.	WHERE IS

FOREIGN MONEY

PRIOR TO EUROS

1.	ARGENTINA		A.	RUPIAHS
2.	AUSTRIA		B.	GUILDERS
3.	BELGIUM		C.	RAND
4.	CHINA		D.	ZLOTY
5.	DENMARK		E.	RUPEES
6.	GERMANY		F.	PESETAS
7.	GREECE		G.	YUAN
8.	HUNGARY		H.	WON
9.	INDONESIA		I.	SHEKELS
10.	ISRAEL		J.	SCHILLINGS
11.	ITALY		K.	RIYAL
12.	JAPAN		L.	DRACHMA
13.	JORDAN		M.	KRONER
14.	KOREA		N.	RINGGITS
15.	MAYLAYSIA		O.	ESCUDOS
16.	NETHERLANDS		P.	MARKS
17.	POLAND		Q.	RUBLES
18.	PORTUGAL		R.	POUNDS
19.	ROMANIA		S.	FORINT
20.	SAUDI ARABIA		T.	YEN
21.	SOUTH AFRICA		U.	LIRA
22.	SPAIN		V.	PESOS
23.	U.K.		W.	DINAR
24.	RUSSIA		X.	BOLIVER
25.	INDIA		Y.	LEI
26.	VENEZULA		Z.	FRANCS

FOREIGN TRAVELS

1.	ABBEY THEATER	A.	AGRA INDIA
2.	DURTY NELLY'S	B.	ALICE SPRINGS, AUSTRALIA
3.	BIG BEN	C.	MADRID, SPAIN
4.	STONEHENGE	D.	SINGAPORE
5.	ARC DE TRIUMPHE	E.	SYDNEY, AUSTRALIA
6.	HALL OF MIRRORS	F.	ROME, ITALY
7.	SISTINE CHAPEL	G.	DUBLIN, IRELAND
8.	TREVI FOUNTAIN	H.	SALISBURY PLAIN, ENGLAND
9.	DACHU	I.	JERUSALEM
10.	THE REICHESTAG	J.	HONG KONG
11.	THE ALHAMBRA	K.	ST. PETERSBURG, RUSSIA
12.	THE PRADO	L.	BERLIN, GERMANY
13.	THE ACROPOLIS	M.	VATICAN CITY
14.	THE HERMITAGE	N.	TOKYO, JAPAN
15.	BONDY BEACH	O.	BEIJING, CHINA
16.	AYERS ROCK	P.	MUNICH, GERMANY
17.	TIGER BALM GARDENS	Q.	PARIS, FRANCE
18.	THE STAR FERRY	R.	RIO DE JANEIRO, BRAZIL
19.	THE GINZA	S.	QUEBEC CITY, PQ, CANADA
20.	THE TAJ MAHAL	T.	VERSAILLES, FRANCE
21.	MOUNT KILIMANJARO	U.	TORONTO, ONT, CANADA
22.	TIANAMEN SQUARE	V.	GRANADA, SPAIN
23.	THE WAILING WALL	W.	LONDON, ENGLAND
24.	CN TOWER	X.	ATHENS GREECE
25.	PLAINS OF ABRAHAM	Y.	SHANNON, IRELAND
26.	IPANEMA BEACH	Z.	TANZANIA, AFRICA

These are the closest well known towns but can be some distance from the named site.

FOREIGN PHRASES

1.	ANNUS MIRABLIS	A.	IN THE ACT
2.	A PRIORI	B.	AN ELUSIVE QUALITY (lit, I do not know what)
3.	AU COURANT	C.	A WITTY REMARK
4.	BONA FIDE	D.	BETWEEN US
5.	BON MOT	E.	FACE TO FACE
6.	BON VIVANT	F.	SO SO
7.	CARPE DIEM	G.	UP TO DATE
8.	CAVEAT EMPTOR	H.	IN WINE THERE IS TRUTH
9.	COMME CI COMME CA	I.	ALREADY DONE
10.	COMME IL FAUT	J.	THE COMMON PEOPLE
11.	COUP DE GRACE	K.	A GREAT YEAR
12.	LA DOLCE VITA	L.	UNWELCOME PERSON
13.	ENFANT TERRIBLE	M.	SOCIAL BLUNDER
14.	ENTRE NOUS	N.	SEIZE THE DAY
15.	FAIT ACCOMPLI	O.	GENUINE
16.	FAUX PAS	P.	I AM AT FAULT
17.	FLAGRANTE DELICTO	Q.	BASED ON THEORY
18.	HOI POLLOI	R.	LET THE BUYER BEWARE
19.	IN LOCO PARENTIS	S.	AT NO CHARGE
20.	IN VINO VERITAS	T.	AS IT SHOULD BE
21.	JE NE SAIS QUOI	U.	VOICE OF THE PEOPLE
22.	MANO A MANO	V.	FINISHING BLOW
23.	MEA CULPA	W.	IN PLACE OF PARENTS
24.	PERSONA NON GRATA	X.	A BRAT
25.	PRO BONO	Y.	THE SWEET LIFE
26.	VOX POPULI	Z.	ONE WHO ENJOYS LIFE

MORE FOREIGN WORDS & PHRASES

1.	AD NAUSEAM	A.	THUS ALWAYS TO TYRANTS
2.	AFICIONADO	B.	RIGHT NOW
3.	BEAU GESTE	C.	UNRESTRICTED POWER OR USE
4.	BETE NOIR	D.	A WAY OF DOING SOMETHING
5.	CARTE BLANCHE	E.	ABILITY TO DO IT RIGHT
6.	CRI DE COEUR	F.	I MAKE AN ACCUSATION
7.	DE RIGUEUR	G.	DISLIKED PERSON OR THING
8.	EX CATHEDRA	H.	TO A SICKENING DEGREE
9.	EX POST FACTO	I.	BY THE FACT
10.	J' ACCUSE	J.	I SAW
11.	IN VITRO	K.	A PEN NAME
12.	IPSO FACTO	L.	ALWAYS FAITHFUL
13.	MODUS OPERANDI	M.	I CAME
14.	NOBLESSE OBLIGE	N.	A DEVOTED FOLLOWER
15.	NOM DE PLUME	O.	I CONQUERED
16.	QUID PRO QUO	P.	FROM THE CHAIR
17.	SAN SOUCI	Q.	CAN'T DO WITHOUT
18.	SEMPER FIDELIS	R.	EVERYONE IN THE WORLD
19.	SIC SEMPER TYRANNIS	S.	IN GLASS
20.	SAVOIR-FAIRE	T.	NOBLE GESTURE
21.	TOUTE DE SUITE	U.	WITHOUT WORRY
22.	TOUTE LE MONDE	V.	APPEAL FROM THE HEART
23.	SINE QUA NON	W.	DUTY TO HELP LESS WELL OFF
24.	VICI	X.	DONE BUT RETROACTIVE
25.	VIDI	Y.	AN EQUAL EXCHANGE
26.	VINI	Z.	REQUIRED BY ETIQUETTE

ALL THINGS MILITARY

1.	ACE	A.	JUNK FOOD OR STORE
2.	ACK-ACK	B.	SNAFU
3.	BULKHEAD	C.	A LIFE JACKET
4.	F-4 PHANTOM	D.	PILOT WITH 5 KILLS
5.	ENOLA GAY	E.	NAVY BOSS PACIFIC FLEET
6.	FATIGUES	F.	SAILORS DAY OFF ASHORE
7.	FLANK	G.	AMERICAN WW2 TANK
8.	FLAT TOP	H.	ARMY/AF BASE STORE
9.	FUBAR	I.	ANTI AIRCRAFT FIRE
10.	CINCPAC	J.	D-DAY PLAN CODE NAME
11.	DEUCE + A HALF	K.	WW2 ARMY RIFLE
12.	GEEDUNK	L.	LARGE HELICOPTER
13.	GITMO	M.	A WALL ON A SHIP
14.	H-1 HUEY	N.	SAILOR WHO HAS CROSSED THE EQUATOR
15.	LIBERTY	O.	JAPANESE WW2 PLANE
16.	JN 25	P.	AIRCRAFT CARRIER
17.	M-1	Q.	ARMY TRUCK
18.	MP'S	R.	WORK UNIFORM
19.	MAE WEST	S.	FASTEST JET EVER
20.	PX	T.	FIGHTER JET (VIETNAM)
21.	SCUTTLEBUTT	U.	JAPANESE NAVAL CODE
22.	SHELLBACK	V.	ENCIRCLING MOTION
23.	OVERLORD	W.	GUANTANAMO BAY CUBA
24.	SR71 BLACKBIRD	X.	THE ARMY'S COPS
25.	SHERMAN	Y.	DROPPED 1ST "A" BOMB
26.	ZERO	Z.	DRINKING FOUNTAIN/NAVY

INVENTORS & DISCOVERERS

1.	IGOR SIKORSKI *	A.	NEUTRON REACTOR
2.	SAMUEL MORSE	B.	ELEVATOR BRAKE
3.	PHILO T. FARNSWORTH	C.	STEAM ENGINE
4.	ELIAS HOWE	D.	BLAST FURNACE
5.	JAMES WATT	E.	AQUALUNG
6.	JETHRO TULL	F.	ASSEMBLY LINE
7.	BEN FRANKLIN	G.	AIR BRAKE
8.	THOMAS EDISON	H.	CAR RADIO & 8 TRACK
9.	GEORGE WESTINGHOUSE	I.	HELICOPTER
10.	ELI WHITNEY	J.	CAST STEEL PLOW
11.	ALEXANDER FLEMING	K.	TV TUBE
12.	HENRY FORD	L.	PHONO GRAPH
13.	HENRY BESSEMER	M.	STABLE BEER
14.	A.G. BELL	N.	VULCANIZED RUBBER
15.	JAQUES COUSTEAU	O.	COTTON GIN
16.	EDWIN LAND	P.	SUPER COMPUTER
17.	G. MARCONI	Q.	SEED PLANTER
18.	JOHN DEERE	R.	ROTARY ENGINE
19.	ROBERT GODDARD	S.	TELPHONE
20.	WILLIAM LEAR	T.	RADIO
21.	E.G. OTIS	U.	INSTANT PICTURES
22.	LOUIS PASTEUR	V.	PENICILLIN
23.	CHAS GOODYEAR	W.	SEWING MACHING
24.	ENRICO FERMI	X.	TELEGRAPH CODE
25.	SEYMOUR CRAY	Y.	BIFOCAL LENSES
26.	FELIX WANKEL	Z.	ROCKET CONTROLS

* WITH OUR APOLOGIES TO OUR OWN MR PITCARIN

IT HAPPENED WHEN?

1.	MAN WALKS ON MOON	A.	1903
2.	FALL OF BERLIN WALL	B.	1908
3.	START OF WW II	C.	1929
4.	DEBUT OF THE EDSEL	D.	1933
5.	DEATH OF JFK	E.	1939
6.	FOUR MINUTE MILE BROKEN	F.	1941
7.	DESERT STORM HITS IRAQ	G.	1944
8.	BEATLES ON ED SULLIVAN	H.	1945
9.	DEATH OF M L KING JR.	I.	1948
10.	REPEAL OF PROHIBITION	J.	1950
11.	FIRST AIRPLANE FLIGHT	K.	1953
12.	PEARL HARBOR ATTACKED	L.	1954
13.	CLINTON IMPEACHED	M.	1957
14.	FIRST HEART TRANSPLANT	N.	1959
15.	STOCK MARKET CRASHES	O.	1963
16.	DEATH OF ELVIS PRESLEY	P.	1964
17.	HAWAII GAINS STATEHOOD	Q.	1967
18.	DEATH OF HRH DIANA	R.	1968
19.	MODEL T INTRODUCED	S.	1969
20.	ELIZABETH II CROWNED	T.	1977
21.	TRUMAN DEFEATS DEWEY	U.	1989
22.	INVASION OF NORMANDY	V.	1991
23.	LANDING AT INCHON	W.	1997
24.	"A" BOMBING OF HIROSHIMA	X.	1998

WHO SAID IT?

1. ASK NOT WHAT YOUR COUNTRY CAN DO FOR YOU
2. I SHALL RETURN
3. GIVE ME LIBERTY OR GIVE DEATH
4. I SHALL GO TO KOREA
5. WE HAVE NOTHING TO FEAR BUT FEAR ITSELF
6. I HAVE NOT YET BEGUN TO FIGHT
7. I AM NOT A CROOK
8. ONE SMALL STEP FOR MAN—
9. I SHALL NOT SEEK AND I WILL NOT ACCEPT MY PARTY'S NOMINATION—
10. NUTS
11. READ MY LIPS, NO NEW TAXES
12. MEN SHALL STILL SAY, THIS WAS THEIR FINEST HOUR
13. IT AIN'T OVER TILL IT'S OVER
14. IF YOU CAN'T STAND THE HEAT GET OUT OF THE KITCHEN
15. THIS WAY TO THE EGRESS
16. MR. GORBACHOV, TEAR DOWN THIS WALL
17. GOV OF THE PEOPLE BY THE PEOPLE FOR THE PEOPLE
18. EARLY TO BED, EARLY TO RISE—.
19. TUNE IN TURN ON DROP OUT
20. SPEAK SOFTLY, AND A CARRY A BIG STICK
21. I FEAR ALL WE HAVE DONE IS AWAKEN A SLEEPING GIANT

A. TIMOTHY LEARY
B. HIDEKI TOJO
C. F. D. ROOSEVELDT
D. YOGI BERRA

E. TEDDY ROOSEVELDT
F. P. T. BARNUM
G. W. A. MCAULIFFE
H. D. D. EISENHOWER

I. JOHN F KENNEDY
J. WINSTON CHURCHILL
K. JIMMY CARTER

L. ABRAHAM LINCOLN
M. RONALD REAGAN

N. WILLIAM CLINTON
O. JOHN PAUL JONES

P. GEORGE H. W. BUSH
Q. DOUGLAS MCARTHUR

R. H. M. STANLEY
S. HARRY TRUMAN

T. RICHARD NIXON

U. LYNDON JOHNSON

22. NOW I HAVE BECOME DEATH

23. I DID NOT HAVE SEX
    WITH THAT WOMAN

24. DR. LIVINGSTONE, I PRESUME

25. I HAVE LUSTED AFTER WOMEN
    IN MY HEART.

26. ON THE WHOLE, I'D RATHER
    BE IN PHILADELPHIA

V. W. C. FIELDS

W. PATRICK HENRY

X. BEN FRANKLIN

Y. NEIL ARMSTRONG

Z. ROBERT OPPENHEIMER

THE BOYS AND GIRLS IN THE BAND

1.	THE MIRACLES	A.	A.J. MCLEAN
2.	THE BEE GEES	B.	MARY WILSON
3.	THE FOUR SEASONS	C.	LINDA RONSTADT
4.	NIRVANA	D.	PETER TORK
5.	THE STONE PONYS	E.	MARLYN MCCOO
6.	THE BELMONTS	F.	STEVEN VAN ZANDT
7.	GUNS AND ROSES	G.	MIX MASTER MIKE
8.	THE UNION GAP	H.	SMOKEY ROBINSON
9.	MAMAS AND PAPAS	I.	LANCE BASS
10.	THE BEATLES	J.	FRANKIE VALLI
11.	THE DIXIE CHICKS	K.	DION DIMUCCI
12.	ROLLING STONES	L.	JOHN FOGERTY
13.	THE MONKEES	M.	SCOTT STAPP
14.	ZZ TOP	N.	OTIS WILLIAMS
15.	THE E STREET BAND	O.	CASS ELLIOT
16.	CREED	P.	WANDA ROGERS
17.	THE MARVELETTES	Q.	GARY PUCKETT
18.	THE TEMPTATIONS	R.	MAURICE GIBB
19.	BACK STREET BOYS	S.	KEITH RICHARDS
20.	THE 5TH DIMENSION	T.	AXEL ROSE
21.	THE SUPREMES	U.	GLEN CAMPBELL
22.	IN SYNC	V.	DUSTY HILL
23.	NO DOUBT	W.	KURT COBAIN
24.	BEASTIE BOYS	X.	EMILY ERWIN
25.	THE BEACH BOYS	Y.	GWEN STEFFANI
26.	CCR	Z.	RICHARD STARKEY

MUSIC VIDEOS

1.	THRILLER	A.	ZZ TOP
2.	MY HEART WILL GO ON	B.	TONY BENNETT
3.	ONE	C.	BILLY JOEL
4.	1979	D.	JANET JACKSON
5.	STEPPIN OUT	E.	DAVID LEE ROTH
6.	SMELLS LIKE TEEN SPIRIT	F.	RADIOHEAD
7.	ADDICTED TO LOVE	G.	MICHAEL JACKSON
8.	IRONIC	H.	CHRISTINA AGUILERA
9.	GIRLS JUST WANT TO HAVE FUN	I.	BON JOVI
10.	WILD THANG	J.	PRINCE
11.	LOVE SHACK	K.	CINDY LAUPER
12.	FREEDOM	L.	SNOOP DOGG
13.	WANTED DEAD/ALIVE	M.	ROBERT PALMER
14.	WHAT A GIRL WANTS	N.	METALLICA
15.	1999	O.	CREED
16.	WHIP IT	P.	CELNIE DION
17.	CANDLE IN THE WIND	Q.	LOST BOYZ
18.	GIMME ALL YOUR LOVIN	R.	TONE LOC
19.	RHYTHM NATION	S.	MADONNA
20.	JUST A GIGOLO	T.	NIRVANA
21.	GIN AND JUICE	U.	GEORGE MICHAEL
22.	UPTOWN GIRL	V.	B 52'S
23.	FAKE PLASTIC TREES	W.	ELTON JOHN
24.	RENEE	X.	DEVO
25.	LIKE A VIRGIN	Y.	ALANIS MORISSETTE
26.	ARMS WIDE OPEN	Z.	SMASHING PUMPKINS

CITIES IN SONGS

1.	I LEFT MY HEART IN	A.	RENO
2.	I'VE GOTTA GIRL IN	B.	NEW YORK
3.	THERE IS A HOUSE IN	C.	BRISTOL
4.	THE LAST TIME I SAW	D.	SAN JOSE
5.	OUT IN THE WEST TEXAS TOWN OF	E.	SAN FRANCISCO
6.	ON THE STREETS OF	F.	PARIS
7.	MY CHINA DOLL DOWN IN OLD	G.	EL PASO
8.	IT'S UP TO YOU	H.	ROMA
9.	THE KIDS IN	I.	HOUSTON
10.	I'M GOING TO	J.	SANTA FE
11.	MIDNITE TRAIN // DESTINATION	K.	CINCINNATI
12.	DO YOU KNOW THE WAY TO	L.	DETROIT CITY
13.	BY THE TIME I GET TO	M.	KALAMAZOO
14.	ON THE ATCHISON, TOPEKA AND	N.	PHILADELPHIA
15.	MY KIND OF TOWN	O.	LAS VEGAS
16.	I SHOT A MAN IN	P.	ST. LOUIS
17.	LAST NITE I WENT TO SLEEP IN	Q.	CAPE MAY
18.	THERE'S 1352 GUITAR PICKERS	R.	NEW ORLEANS
19.	ON THE WAY TO	S.	MEMPHIS
20.	GOING BACK TO	T.	KANSAS CITY
21.	PARDON ME BOY, IS THAT THE	U.	PHOENIX
22.	MEET ME IN	V.	NASHVILLE
23.	ARRIVEDERCI	W.	CHATTANOOGA
24.	HELP ME INFORMATION, GET ME	X.	HONG KONG
25.	I'M AT WKRP IN	Y.	BANGOR (MAINE)
26.	VIVA	Z.	CHICAGO

WW2 ERA SONGS

1.	WHEN YOU WISH UPON A STAR	A.	OLD FAMILIAR PLACES
2.	CHATTANOOGA CHOO CHOO	B.	KISS ME TWICE
3.	DEEP IN THE HEART OF TEXAS	C.	MISTER IN BETWEEN
4.	DON'T SIT UNDER THE APPLE TREE	D.	WE DRINK IT HERE
5.	WHITE CLIFFS OF DOVER	E.	FINE TOOTH COMB
6.	AS TIME GOES BY	F.	HAUNTS MY REVERIE
7.	PAPER DOLL	G.	BLUEBIRDS OVER
8.	DON'T FENCE ME IN	H.	WHITE WITH FOAM
9.	I'LL BE SEEING YOU	I.	HOW LOVELY IT WAS
10.	MAIRZY DOATS	J.	PARDON ME, BOY
11.	SWINGING ON A STAR	K.	TWO LOVERS WOO
12.	IT'S BEEN A LONG LONG TIME	L.	SODA + PRETZELS + BEER
13.	RUM AND COCA-COLA	M.	WILL COME TO YOU
14.	SENTIMENTAL JOURNEY	N.	TO ONE HUNDRED + FIVE
15.	AC-CENT-TCHU-ATE THE POSTIVE	O.	FLIRTY FLIRTY EYES
16.	WHITE CHRISTMAS	P.	IN YOUR POCKET
17.	OVER THE RAINBOW	Q.	TIL I COME MARCHIN HOME
18.	THANKS FOR THE MEMORY	R.	RATHER BE A MULE
19.	BILL BAILEY	S.	BIG AND BRIGHT
20.	CATCH A FALLING STAR	T.	UNDERN'TH THE LAMPLITE
21.	IN HEAVEN THERE IS NO	U.	GONNA TAKE A
22.	STARDUST	V.	STARRY SKIES ABOVE
23.	THOSE LAZY HAZY CRAZY DAYS	W.	IN A LULLABY
24.	YOUNG AT HEART	X.	LAMBS EAT IVY
25.	LILY MARLENE	Y.	CHILDREN LISTEN
26.	GOD BLESS AMERICA	Z.	YANKEE DOLLAR

MERRY CHRISTMAS JOYEUX NOEL

1.	SILENT NIGHT	A.	WHERE OX & ASS ARE FEEDING
2.	HARK THE HERALD ANGELS	B.	AND EVERYWHERE
3.	O COME ALL YE FAITHFUL	C.	RECIEVE HER KING
4.	THE FIRST NOEL	D.	TAIL AS BIG AS A KITE
5.	GO TELL IT ON THE MOUNTAIN	E.	STOOD A LOWLY CATTLE SHED
6.	LITTLE DRUMMER BOY	F.	AND MERCY MILD
7.	O LITTLE TOWN OF BETHLEHEM	G.	HE SHALL REIGN FOREVER
8.	COME TO THE MANGER	H.	ON CHRISTMAS DAY IN THE MORNING
9.	HANDEL'S MESSIAH	I.	WEARY WORLD REJOICES
10.	WHAT CHILD IS THIS	J.	HE LIES 'MID THE BEASTS
11.	GOD REST YOU MERRY, GENTLEMAN	K.	CERTAIN POOR SHEPHERDS
12.	ANGELS WE HAVE HEARD	L.	ROUND YON VIRGIN
13.	AWAY IN A MANGER	M.	STAR OF WONDER, STAR OF NIGHT
14.	IT CAME UPON A MIDNIGHT CLEAR	N.	AND RANSOM CAPTIVE ISRAEL
15.	RISE UP SHEPHERD	O.	TO SAVE US ALL
16.	ANGELS FROM THE REALMS OF GLORY	P.	WHEN MARY BIRTHED JESUS
17.	GOOD KING WENCESLAS	Q.	ASLEEP ON THE HAY
18.	I SAW THREE SHIPS	R.	HARPS OF GOLD
19.	JOY TO THE WORLD	S.	ANCIENT YULETIDE CAROL
20.	O HOLY NIGHT	T.	DEEP & CRISP & EVEN
21.	DO YOU HEAR WHAT I HEAR	U.	I HAVE NO GIFT TO BRING
22.	I WONDER AS I WANDER	V.	SAINTS BEFORE THE ALTAR BENDING

23. O COME O COME EMANUEL
24. DECK THE HALLS

25. WE THREE KINGS
26. ONCE IN DAVID'S ROYAL CITY

W. THE EVERLASTING LIGHT
X. YOU'LL FORGET YOUR FLOCKS
Y. JOYFUL & TRIUMPHANT
Z. IN EXCELSIS DEO

MERRY CHRISTMAS (NOT RELIGIOUS)

1.	BLUE CHRISTMAS	A.	HURRY DOWN THE CHIMNEY
2.	FROSTY THE SNOWMAN	B.	CORN FOR POPPING
3.	HAVE YOURSELF A MERRY	C.	A HULA HOOP
4.	HERE COMES SANTA CLAUSE	D.	BETTER NOT POUT
5.	HOLLY JOLLY CHRISTMAS	E.	DECORATIONS OF RED
6.	I SAW MOMMY KISSING SANTA	F.	IN THE FIVE AND TEN
7.	I'LL BE HOME FOR XMAS	G.	CALLING YOU HOO
8.	IT'S BEGINNING TO LOOK	H.	DRESSED IN HOLIDAY STYLE
9.	LET IT SNOW	I.	FAITHFUL ARE THY BRANCHES
10.	ROCKING AROUND	J.	CUDDLY AS A CACTUS
11.	RUDOLPH THE RED NOSED	K.	CAME TO LIFE ONE DAY
12.	SANTA BABY	L.	SANTA CLAUS LANE
13.	SANTA CLAUS IS COMING	M.	DANCIN' AND PRANCIN'
14.	SILVER BELLS	N.	GLAD TIDINGS WE BRING
15.	SLEIGH RIDE	O.	IF I COULD ONLY WHISTLE
16.	WHITE CHRISTMAS	P.	CHRISTMAS PARTY HOP
17.	WINTER WONDERLAND	Q.	IF ONLY IN MY DREAMS
18.	ALL I WANT FOR XMAS	R.	YULETIDE CAROLS
19.	THE CHIPMUNK SONG	S.	LADIES DANCING
20.	THE CHRISTMAS SONG	T.	DADDY HAD ONLY SEEN
21.	WE WISH YOU A MERRY CHRISTMAS	U.	IN THE MEADOW
22.	GRANDMA GOT RUN OVER	V.	HAVE A CUP OF CHEER
23.	THE GRINCH	W.	WILL BE MILES AWAY
24.	THE 12 DAYS OF XMAS	X.	DOWN IN HISTORY
25.	O CHRISTMAS TREE	Y.	NO SUCH THING AS SANTA
26.	JINGLE BELL ROCK	Z.	TREETOPS GLISTEN

U.S. VICE PRESIDENTS

1.	GEORGE WASHINGTON		A.	RICHARD CHENEY
2.	ZACHARY TAYLOR		B.	ALBEN BARKLEY
3.	JOHN F. KENNEDY		C.	CHESTER A ARTHUR
4.	JOHN ADAMS		D.	HENRY WILSON
5.	RONALD REAGAN		E.	TEDDY ROOSEVELT
6.	ABE LINCOLN		F.	HARRY TRUMAN
7.	JIMMY CARTER		G.	ADALI STEVENSON
8.	WARREN G. HARDING		H.	MILLARD FILMORE
9.	HARRY TRUMAN		I.	SPIRO T AGNEW
10.	THOMAS JEFFERSON		J.	ELBRIDGE GERRY
11.	WM. MCKINLEY		K.	JOHN ADAMS
12.	LYNDON JOHNSON		L.	JOHN TYLER
13.	JAMES A GARFIELD		M.	NONE
14.	DWIGHT EISENHOWER		N.	ALBERT GORE JR.
15.	WM HENRY HARRISON		O.	LYNDON JOHNSON
16.	FRANKLIN ROOSEVELT		P.	GEORGE H.W. BUSH
17.	GEORGE W. BUSH		Q.	WALTER MONDALE
18.	GERALD FORD		R.	J DANFORTH QUAYLE
19.	ANDREW JOHNSON		S.	JOHN C. CALHOUN
20.	RICHARD M NIXON		T.	AARON BURR
21.	JAMES MADISON		U.	RICHARD NIXON
22.	GEORGE H. W. BUSH		V.	ANDREW JOHNSON
23.	JOHN QUINCY ADAMS		W.	NELSON ROCKEFELLER
24.	GROVER CLEVELAND		X.	CALVIN COOLIDGE
25.	ULYSSES S. GRANT		Y.	THOMAS JEFFERSON
26.	WILLIAM CLINTON		Z.	HUBERT HUMPHREY

U.S. SENATORS THEN & NOW

1.	BARRY GOLDWATER	A.	GEORGIA
2.	DANIEL INOUYE	B.	NEW JERSEY
3.	RICHARD NIXON	C.	UTAH
4.	EVERETT M. DIRKSEN	D.	MAINE
5.	ORIN HATCH	E.	WYOMING
6.	LYNDON B JOHNSON	F.	WISCONSIN
7.	CONNIE MACK	G.	ILLNOIS
8.	BARBARA MIKULSKI	H.	ARIZONA
9.	FRED THOMPSON	I.	LOUISIANA
10.	JACOB JAVITS	J.	OHIO
11.	GARY HART	K.	CALIFORNIA
12.	HUEY LONG	L.	RHODE ISLAND
13.	MARGARET CHASE SMITH	M.	DELAWARE
14.	JOHN F. KENNEDY	N.	ARKANSAS
15.	JOE MCCARTHY	O.	COLORADO
16.	NANCY LANDON KASSEBAUM	P.	HAWAII
17.	STROM THURMOND	Q.	NEW YORK
18.	CLAIBORNE PELL	R.	WEST VIRGINIA
19.	SAM NUNN	S.	TENNESEE
20.	ALAN SIMPSON	T.	MASSACHUSETTS
21.	BILL BRADLEY	U.	MINNESOTA
22.	HATTIE WYATT CARAWAY	V.	FLORIDA
23.	HUBERT H HUMPHREY	W.	KANSAS
24.	ROBERT BYRD	X.	SOUTH CAROLINA
25.	JOHN GLENN	Y.	MARYLAND
26.	WILLIAM ROTH	Z.	TEXAS

FAMOUS PAIRS

1. LEWIS AND
2. BURNS AND
3. ROGERS AND
4. SACCO AND
5. MARTIN AND
6. HORN AND
7. SIMON AND
8. BINNEY AND
9. ABERCROMBIE AND
10. ABBOTT AND
11. LEA AND
12. FERRANTE AND
13. LEOPOLD AND
14. SEARS AND
15. CURRIER AND
16. DUN AND
17. MARTINI AND
18. GILBERT AND
19. BROOKS AND
20. LERNER AND
21. JUSTERINI AND
22. SISKEL AND
23. MASTERS AND
24. MASON AND
25. PENN AND
26. CRICK AND

A. COSTELLO
B. IVES
C. SMITH
D. ROEBUCK
E. LOEB
F. VANZETTI
G. CLARK
H. EBERT
I. LEWIS
J. TELLER
K. LOEWE
L. ROSSI
M. WATSON
N. SULLIVAN
O. PERRINS
P. DIXON
Q. FITCH
R. HAMMERSTEIN
S. JOHNSON
T. ALLEN
U. BRADSTREET
V. TEICHER
W. HARDART
X. BROOKS
Y. GARFUNKEL
Z. DUNN

ALSO KNOWN AS

1.	MARION MICHAEL MORRISON	A.	MARILYN MONROE
2.	NATHAN BIRNBAUM	B.	ALAN ALDA
3.	SAMUEL LANGHORN CLEMENS	C.	JOHN WAYNE
4.	HENRY JOHN DEUTSCHENDORF JR.	D.	CHER
5.	CARYN JOHNSON	E.	TOM CRUISE
6.	ARCHIBALD LEACH	F.	ELTON JOHN
7.	FERDINAND L. ALCINDOR JR.	G.	WOODY ALLEN
8.	ALPHONSO D'ABRUZZO	H.	AHMAD RASHAD
9.	ALLEN KONIGSBERG	I.	POPE JOHN PAUL II
10.	ERNEST EVANS	J.	KAREEM ABDUL JABBAR
11.	THOMAS MAPOTHER 4TH.	K.	JOHN DENVER
12.	ROBERT ZIMMERMAN	L.	ALICE COOPER
13.	CASSIUS MARCELLUS CLAY JR.	M.	CARY GRANT
14.	CHERILYN SARKISIAN	N.	GERALD FORD
15.	BERNARD SCHWARTZ	O.	BOB HOPE
16.	FRANCES GUMM	P.	GEORGE BURNS
17.	GORDON SUMMER	Q.	RINGO STARR
18.	LESLIE TOWNES HOPE	R.	TONY CURTIS
19.	REGINALD DWIGHT	S.	STING
20.	NORMA JEAN BAKER	T.	MUHAMMAD ALI
21.	BOBBY MOORE	U.	WHOOPI GOLDBERG
22.	CARLOS IRWIN ESTEVEZ	V.	MARK TWAIN
23.	RICHARD STARKEY	W.	BOB DYLAN
24.	KAROL WOJTYLA	X.	CHUBBY CHECKER
25.	VINCENT DAMON FURRIER	Y.	JUDY GARLAND
26.	LESLIE LYNCH KING JR.	Z.	CHARLIE SHEEN

ODD JOB TITLES

1.	ARBITRAGEUR	A.	MAKES WOMENS HATS
2.	BARRISTER	B.	CIRCUS LABORER
3.	BEEFEATER	C.	MAP MAKER
4.	CANINE PERAMBULATOR	D.	MOVES MOVIE SET EQUIPMENT
5.	CARTOGRAPHER	E.	BOXER
6.	CHIROPODIST	F.	PENS WORDS FOR SONGS
7.	CONCIERGE	G.	MAKE UP ARTIST
8.	COOPER	H.	DOG WALKER
9.	CROUPIER	I.	BUY/SELLS STOCKS
10.	COSMETICIAN	J.	MENS CLOTHIER
11.	GANDY DANCER	K.	WINE MAKER
12.	HABERDASHER	L.	BARTENDER
13.	KEY GRIP	M.	U.S. NAVY CLERK
14.	LAPIDARY	N.	RAIL ROAD CREW WORKER
15.	LYRICIST	O.	MANAGES A GAMING TABLE
16.	MIXOLOGIST	P.	ACTOR
17.	OCULIST	Q.	FOOT DOCTOR
18.	ONCOLOGIST	R.	LADY OF ILL REPUTE
19.	MILLINER	S.	COURTROOM ATTORNEY
20.	PUGILIST	T.	HOTEL HEAD PORTER
21.	ROUSTABOUT	U.	EYE DOCTOR
22.	SOMMELIER	V.	JEWLER
23.	STRUMPET	W.	BARREL MAKER
24.	THESPIAN	X.	TOWER OF LONDON GUARD
25.	VINTNER	Y.	WINE STEWARD
26.	YEOMAN	Z.	CANCER DOCTOR

MATCH THE AUTHOR WITH THE WORK

1. THE OLD MAN & THE SEA
2. DON QUIXOTE
3. TREASURE ISLAND
4. MOBY DICK
5. SHOGUN
6. JAYNE AYRE
7. ALICE IN WONDERLAND
8. THE GOOD EARTH
9. HUNT FOR RED OCTOBER
10. JURRASIC PARK
11. TALES OF THE SOUTH PACIFIC
12. THE WINDS OF WAR
13. AROUND THE WORLD IN 80 DAYS
14. ADVENTURES OF TOM SAWYER
15. PROFILES IN COURAGE
16. CANTERBURY TALES
17. HUNCHBACK OF NOTRE DAME
18. SILENT SPRING
19. THE TIME MACHINE
20. THE FALL/HOUSE OF USHER
21. CATCH 22
22. PRIDE & PREJUDICE
23. CATCHER IN THE RYE
24. THE HOBBIT
25. ANIMAL FARM
26. T/GRASS IS ALWAYS GREENER

A. V. HUGO
B. J. F. KENNEDY
C. R. CARSON
D. J. CLAVELL
E. E. HEMMINGWAY
F. H. MELVILLE
G. T. CLANCY
H. M. TWAIN
I. L. CARROLL
J. H.G. WELLS
K. E. BRONTE
L. J. HELLER
M. G. ORWELL
N. E. A. POE
O. J. AUSTEN
P. M. CERVANTES
Q. M. CRICHTON
R. J. R. R. TOLKIEN
S. E. BOMBECK
T. J. VERNE
U. H. WOUK
V. J. D. SALINGER
W. J. MICHENER
X. R. L. STEVENSON
Y. P. S. BUCK
Z. G. CHAUCER

(OVER THE SEPTIC TANK)

62

COMPOSERS

1.	JOHN PHILLIP SOUSA	A.	ODE TO JOY (NINTH SYMPHONY)
2.	WOLFGANG MOZART	B.	GOD BLESS AMERICA
3.	AARON COPELAND	C.	THEME FROM MOVIE JAWS
4.	LUDWIG VON BEETHOVEN	D.	THE MAPLE LEAF RAG
5.	STEPHEN FOSTER	E.	LA TRAVIATA
6.	JOHANNES BRAHMS	F.	THE WILLIAM TELL OVERTURE
7.	HENRY MANCINI	G.	HUNGARIAN RHAPSODY #12
8.	J. S. BACH	H.	THE STARS AND STRIPES FOREVER
9.	JOHN WILLIAMS	I.	SLEIGH RIDE
10.	JOHANN STRAUSS II	J.	PEER GYNT SUITES
11.	LEROY ANDERSON	K.	NESSUM DORMA
12.	ANTONIO VIVALDI	L.	EINE KLINE NACHTMUSIK
13.	GEORGE GERSHWIN	M.	MOON RIVER
14.	CLAUDE DEBUSSY	N.	THE TOREADOR'S SONG
15.	RICHARD WAGNER	O.	MY OLD KENTUCKY HOME
16.	SCOTT JOPLIN	P.	THE BLUE DANUBE
17.	PETER TCHAIKOWSKY	Q.	THE FOUR SEASONS
18.	FRANZ LISZT	R.	GERMAN REQUIEM
19.	ALEXANDER BORODIN	S.	BOLERO
20.	EDVARD GRIEG	T.	TRISTAN AND ISOLADE
21.	GEORGE BIZET	U.	HOEDOWN (FROM RODEO)
22.	GUISEPPE VERDI	V.	RHAPSODY IN BLUE
23.	GIOACCHINO ROSSINI	W.	THE 1812 OVERTURE
24.	MAURICE RAVEL	X.	CLARE DE LUNE
25.	GIACOMO PUCCINI	Y.	TOCCATA & FUGUE IN D
26.	IRVING BERLIN	Z.	POLOVTSIAN DANCES

A SAILORS VOCABULARY

1.	AFT	A.	DEPTH OF A SHIP IN WATER
2.	AMIDSHIPS	B.	ONE WHO SUPPLIES SHIPS
3.	BALLAST	C.	PORTABLE WALKWAY TO GO ABOARD
4.	BARGE	D.	TO HAUL UP (ESP THE ANCHOR)
5.	BEAM	E.	POWERFUL SMALL BOAT
6.	BOATSWAIN	F.	DESIGNED TO JUST FIT PANAMA CANAL
7.	BRIDGE	G.	RAISED FRONT PART OF THE DECK
8.	BULKHEAD	H.	DO NOT OVERLOAD LINE
9.	CHANDLER	I.	A LARGE ROPE
10.	COLLIER	J.	FLAT BOTTOM CARGO CARRIER
11.	DAVITS	K.	TOWARDS THE REAR OF THE SHIP
12.	DRAFT	L.	SUDDEN VIOLENT WIND OR STORM
13.	FORCASTLE	M.	WHERE THE CAPTAIN STEERS FROM
14.	GANGWAY	N.	VESSEL TO TRANSPORT COAL
15.	GUNWALE	O.	BOSS OF ALL DECK HANDS
16.	HAWSER	P.	DEVICE A LIFEBOAT HANGS FROM
17.	INTERMODAL	Q.	THE RIGHT SIDE OF THE SHIP
18.	KNOT	R.	CARVINGS IN SHELL OR WHALEBONE
19.	PANAMAX	S.	IN THE MIDDLE OF THE SHIP
20.	PLIMSOL LINE	T.	THE WIDTH OF THE SHIP
21.	QUAY	U.	MEASUREMENT OF SPEED
22.	SCRIMSHAW	V.	HIGHEST SIDE BOARD OF SHIP
23.	SQUALL	W.	A WALL OF A SHIP
24.	STARBOARD	X.	WHARF USED TO LOAD OR UNLOAD
25.	TUG	Y.	EXTRA WEIGHT FOR STABILITY
26.	WEIGH	Z.	USING MORE THAN 1 TYPE OF TRANSPORT

A WORKING VOCABULARY

1.	BLACKSMITH	A.	JEROBOAM
2.	PILOT	B.	LARIAT
3.	SHIPWRIGHT	C.	ONOMATOPOEIA
4.	CHEF	D.	BRIS
5.	POET	E.	JAKE BRAKE
6.	SHEPHERD	F.	METRONOME
7.	DRAFTSMAN	G.	HECTARE
8.	BARTENDER	H.	STENT
9.	PRINTER	I.	ANVIL
10.	MOHEL	J.	SCRIMSHAW
11.	FLY FISHERMAN	K.	MOSTRANCE
12.	POTTER	L.	HOD
13.	SAILOR	M.	ALTIMETER
14.	HABBERDASHER	N.	CROOK
15.	TRUCKER	O.	CLEAVER
16.	ROMAN CATHOLIC PRIEST	P.	PLECTRUM
17.	POLITICIAN	Q.	FUTTOCK
18.	FARMER	R.	EM
19.	SOMMELIER	S.	KILN
20.	BUTCHER	T.	JIGGER
21.	COWBOY	U.	TOQUE BLANCHE
22.	PC PROGRAMMER	V.	CREEL
23.	CUITAR PLAYER	W.	PROTRACTOR
24.	SURGEON	X.	FORTRAN
25.	PIANIST	Y.	GERRYMANDER
26.	BRICKLAYER	Z.	CUMMERBUND

THE FUNNY PAPERS

1.	DOONESBURY	A.	TED KEY
2.	PEANUTS	B.	BRANT PARKER
3.	NANCY	C.	JIM DAVIS
4.	CATHY	D.	BILL WATTERSON
5.	GARFIELD	E.	HANK KETCHAM
6.	FAMILY CIRCUS	F.	J & C BENDER
7.	DICK TRACY	G.	GREG EVANS
8.	HAGAR THE HORRIBLE	H.	HORST & REINER
9.	BLONDIE	I.	JOHNNY HART
10.	CALVIN & HOBBS	J.	GARY TRUDEAU
11.	BEATLE BAILEY	K.	C. GUISEWITE
12.	ALLEY OOP	L.	BRAD ANDERSON
13.	THE LOCKHORNS	M.	GARY LARSON
14.	BRENDA STARR	N.	BIL KEANE
15.	DENNIS THE MENACE	O.	AL CAPP
16.	DILBERT	P.	CHESTER GOULD
17.	ANDY CAPP	Q.	CHIC YOUNG
18.	GASOLINE ALLEY	R.	CHARLES SCHULTZ
19.	HAZEL	S.	BOB THAVES
20.	THE FAR SIDE	T.	BRIGMAN & SCHMICH
21.	WIZARD OF ID	U.	MORT WALKER
22.	BC	V.	REG SMYTHE
23.	FRANK & ERNEST	W.	G & B GILCHRIST
24.	MARMADUKE	X.	SCOTT ADAMS
25.	LUANN	Y.	CHRIS BROWNE
26.	LIL ABNER	Z.	FRANK KING

GAMES PEOPLE PLAY

1.	MONOPOLY	A.	NAUGHTY DEEDS
2.	CHECKERS	B.	THE CONSERVATORY
3.	CANASTA	C.	DASHER
4.	SCRABBLE	D.	KAMCHATKA
5.	CLUE	E.	MARBLES
6.	POKEMON	F.	THE WIZARD
7.	CHESS	G.	TOWER
8.	PINOCHLE	H.	GINGERBREAD HOUSE
9.	RISK	I.	SEVEN CARD MELD
10.	POKER	J.	20 SIDED DIE
11.	20 QUESTIONS	K.	SPOUSE
12.	PARCHEESI	L.	DO NOT PASS GO
13.	CHUTES & LADDERS	M.	PIE WEDGE
14.	CHINESE CHECKERS	N.	KING ME
15.	BACKGAMMON	O.	A NATURAL
16.	BOGGLE	P.	HOME PATH
17.	CANDYLAND	Q.	MUGGINS
18.	SCATTERGORIES	R.	EN PASSANT
19.	JENGA	S.	TRIPLE WORD VALUE
20.	BACCARAT	T.	ROYAL FLUSH
21.	MAH JONGG	U.	PIKACHU
22.	BALDERDASH	V.	DOME
23.	TRIVIAL PURSUIT	W.	A BREAD BOX
24.	DOMINOES	X.	WALL OF TILES
25.	LIFE	Y.	BLOT
26.	DUNGEONS AND DRAGONS	Z.	JACK OF DIAMONDS / QUEEN OF SPADES

FOR REAL SPORTS

1.	GREEN BAY	A.	THRASHERS
2.	DALLAS	B.	RAVENS
3.	KANSAS CITY	C.	STING
4.	MIAMI	D.	DEVIL RAYS
5.	JACKSONVILLE	E.	RAPTORS
6.	PHILADELPHIA	F.	PACKERS
7.	BALTIMORE	G.	PREDATORS
8.	BUFFALO	H.	HEAT
9.	TENNESSEE	I.	WAVE
10.	ATLANTA	J.	JAGUARS
11.	HOUSTON	K.	ATTACK
12.	MILWAUKEE	L.	WILD
13.	TORNOTO	M.	SHOCK
14.	PHOENIX	N.	TITANS
15.	TAMPA BAY	O.	ROCKETS
16.	OTTAWA	P.	LAND SHARKS
17.	SAN DIEGO	Q.	KIXX
18.	MINNESOTA	R.	REDSKINS
19.	NASHVILLE	S.	COMETS
20.	CHARLOTTE	T.	ROYALS
21.	WICHITA	U.	SPIRIT
22.	COLUMBUS	V.	STARS
23.	WASHINGTON	W.	WINGS
24.	DETROIT	X.	REBEL
25.	ALBANY	Y.	COYOTES
26.	CLEVELAND	Z.	BLIZZARD

SPORTS STARS PAST

1.	BEN HOGAN	A.	DECATHALON
2.	PEGGY FLEMING	B.	GOLF (F)
3.	INGEMAR JOHANSSON	C.	BOWLING
4.	RAFER JOHNSON	D.	DOG SLED RACING
5.	STEVE CAUTHEN	E.	GOLF (M)
6.	JESSE OWENS	F.	BASEBALL (AL)
7.	MAUREEN CONNOLLY	G.	AEROBATIC FLYING
8.	JACKIE STEWART	H.	ICE HOCKEY
9.	MARY DECKER	I.	FOOTBALL
10.	ROGERS HORNSBY	J.	BOXING
11.	NADIA COMANNECI	K.	TRACK & FIELD (M)
12.	PETE MARAVICH	L.	SKIING (M)
13.	SUSAN BUTCHER	M.	FIGURE SKATING (F)
14.	DICK WEBER	N.	DIVING
15.	JUDY RANKIN	O.	HORSE RACING (SULKY)
16.	JOE DALEY*	P.	SKIING (F)
17.	HARMON KILLABREW	Q.	GYMNASTICS (F)
18.	BRONKO NAGURSKI	R.	TENNIS (M)
19.	STANLEY DANCER	S.	TRACK & FIELD (F)
20.	GREG LUGANIS	T.	FIGURE SKATING (M)
21.	PICABO STREET	U.	BASKETBALL
22.	STAN SMITH	V.	SMIMMING
23.	PATTI WAGSTAFF	W.	GRAN PRIX RACING
24.	SCOTT HAMILTON	X.	BASEBALL (NL)
25.	MARK SPITZ	Y.	HORSERACING (FLAT)
26.	J.C. KILLY	Z.	TENNIS (F)

* No relation to the author of this quiz.

SPORTS VENUES

1.	ANAHEIM, CA	A.	SOLDIER FIELD
2.	BALTIMORE, MD	B.	MC NICHOLS ARENA
3.	BOSTON, MA	C.	LAMBEAU FIELD
4.	CHICAGO, IL	D.	ARROWHEAD STADIUM
5.	CLEVELAND, OH	E.	ARROWNHEAD POND
6.	DENVER, CO	F.	OLYMPIC STADIUM
7.	DETROIT, MI	G.	CAMDEN YARDS
8.	EDMONTON, AL	H.	JACOBS FIELDS
9.	GREEN BAY, WI	I.	MARKET SQUARE ARENA
10.	INDIANAPOLIS	J.	JOE LEWIS ARENA
11.	KANSAS CITY, MO	K.	SKY REACH CENTRE
12.	MONTREAL, PQ	L.	FENWAY PARK
13.	NYC (FLUSHING), NY	M.	QUALCOM STADIUM
14.	UNIONDALE, (LI), NY	N.	THREE RIVERS STADIUM
15.	KANATA, ON	O.	SHEA STADIUM
16.	PHILADELPHIA, PA	P.	3 COM STADIUM
17.	PITTSBURGH, PA	Q.	NASSAU COLISEUM
18.	PORTLAND, OR	R.	ADELPHIA STADIUM
19.	ST. LOUIS, MO	S.	VETERNS STADIUM
20.	SAN DIEGO, CA	T.	JACK KENT COOKE STA
21.	SAN FRANCISCO, CA	U.	COREL CENTRE
22.	NASHVILLE, TN	V.	ROSE GARDEN
23.	WASHINGTON, DC	W.	BUSCH STADIUM

NOTE: Some are gone some have changed names.

SPORTS TERMS

1.	BALK	A.	SHOOTING
2.	TURKEY	B.	BASKETBALL
3.	WICKET	C.	ROCK CLIMBING
4.	SCRUM	D.	TENNIS
5.	FLETCH	E.	WEIGHTLIFTING
6.	FRONTON	F.	SKATING
7.	SILKS	G.	SOCCER
8.	BONSPIEL	H.	RUGBY
9.	MASHIE	I.	BASEBALL
10.	CORNER KICK	J.	AEROBATICS
11.	GRIDIRON	K.	FISHING
12.	PARRY	L.	WRESTLING
13.	LOVE	M.	HOCKEY
14.	BOWSPRIT	N.	BADMINTON
15.	DOUBLE AXEL	O.	FENCING
16.	RACK	P.	CRICKET
17.	ZAMBONI	Q.	JAI ALAI
18.	SINGLET	R.	BOWLING
19.	RIMFIRE	S.	ARCHERY
20.	DEAD LIFT	T.	POOL
21.	SHOT CLOCK	U.	GOLF
22.	CARABINER	V.	SAILING
23.	CREEL	W.	FOOTBALL
24.	RESTRICTOR PLATE	X.	HORSE RACING
25.	SHUTTLECOCK	Y.	CURLING
26.	IMMELMANN	Z.	AUTO RACING

SPORTS NICKNAMES

1.	THE BABE	A.	MUHAMMAD ALI
2.	THE GOLDEN JET	B.	EARL MONROE
3.	SPLENDID SPLINTER	C.	REGGIE JACKSON
4.	THE SHARK	D.	TONY ESPOSITO
5.	THE MAILMAN	E.	JACK NICKLAUS
6.	THE BULL	F.	WILLIAM PERRY
7.	MODERN MR ZERO	G.	WAYNE GRETZKY
8.	MR. OCTOBER	H.	RANDY JOHNSON
9.	THE CYCLONE (CY)	I.	OSCAR ROBERTSON
10.	THE HAMMER	J.	WILLIE MAYS
11.	THE SNAKE	K.	KARL MALONE
12.	CHARLIE HUSTLE	L.	O.J. SIMPSON
13.	THE BIG O	M.	TOMMY HEARNS
14.	BOOM BOOM	N.	KEN STABLER
15.	THE REFRIGERATOR	O.	BOBBY HULL
16.	THE LOUISVILLE LIP	P.	PETE ROSE
17.	THE ROCKET	Q.	JOE DIMAGGIO
18.	THE JUICE	R.	DENTON YOUNG
19.	THE BIG UNIT	S.	TED WILLIAMS
20.	THE ICEMAN	T.	DAVE SHULTZ
21.	THE GREAT ONE	U.	GEORGE HERMAN RUTH
22.	THE HITMAN	V.	BERNIE GEOFFRION
23.	THE PEARL	W.	GEORGE GERVIN
24.	THE GOLDEN BEAR	X.	GREG NORMAN
25.	THE SAY HEY KID	Y.	MAURICE RICHARD
26.	YANKEE CLIPPER	Z.	GREG LUZINSKI

BUILDINGS KNOWN BY NAME

1. FALLINGWATER
2. BLACK ROCK
3. MONTICELLO
4. SCOTTY'S CASTLE
5. DRUMTHWACKET
6. THE HOUSE THAT RUTH BUILT
7. THE HERMITAGE
8. THE BREAKERS
9. THE CASTLE
10. GRACIE MANSION

11. MOUNT VERNON
12. PICKFAIR

13. CHARTWELL
14. IOLANI PALACE
15. TERRACE HILL

16. ORCHARD HOUSE
17. FAIRLANE
18. U. S. NAVAL OBSERVATORY
19. GRACELAND
20. BEEHIVE HOUSE
21. ARROWHEAD
22. CASTLE GANDOLFO

23. HAUS WACHENFELD
24. THE OLD LADY OF THREADNEEDLE ST.

A. RESIDENCE OF D. FAIRBANKS & M. PICKFORD
B. SMITHSONIAN INST. ADMIN. OFFICES
C. HOME OF ELVIS PRESLEY
D. HOME BY FRANK LLOYD WRIGHT
E. ESTATE OF WINSTON CHURCHILL

F. THE VANDERBILT COTTAGE
G. GOVERNOR'S MANSION, IOWA
H. ONLY ROYAL RESIDENCE IN THE US
I. HITLER'S MOUNTAIN HOME
J. H. MELVILLE FINISHED MOBY DICK HERE
K. GOVERNORS MANSION, NJ
L. OFFICIAL RESIDENCE OF BRIGHAM YOUNG
M. MANSION IN DEATH VALLEY
N. THE BANK OF ENGLAND
O. OFFICIAL RESIDENCE OF THE US VICE PRESIDENT
P. SUMMER HOME OF THE POPE
Q. YANKEE STADIUM
R. HOME OF THOMAS JEFFERSON
S. ESTATE OF GEORGE WASHINGTON
T. CBS HEADQUARTERS
U. ESTATE OF HENRY FORD
V. L. M. ALCOTT WROTE LITTLE WOMEN HERE
W. MAYORS MANSION, NEW YORK CITY
X. HOME OF ANDREW JACKSON

ATOMS AND MOLECULES

1.	AS	A.	TIN
2.	AU	B.	SAND
3.	C	C.	WATER
4.	CA	D.	ARGON
5.	CU	E.	HYDROGEN
6.	CAO	F.	HYDROGEN PEROXIDE
7.	CH4	G.	ARSNIC
8.	CO2	H.	POTASSIUM
9.	Fe	I.	TUNGSTEN
10.	Ar	J.	LEAD
11.	Ag	K.	CARBON
12.	Pb	L.	LIME
13.	Hg	M.	COPPER
14.	H	N.	IODINE
15.	Na	O.	PHOSPHORUS
16.	Sn	P.	IRON
17.	I	Q.	METHANE
18.	W	R.	TITANIUM
19.	H20	S.	MERCURY
20.	SiO2	T.	CHLORINE
21.	NaCl	U.	SILVER
22.	H202	V.	SODIUM
23.	K	W.	GOLD
24.	P	X.	CALCIUM
25.	Ti	Y.	SALT
26.	Cl	Z.	CARBON DIOXIDE

MEASURING UP

1.	FATHOMS	A.	ELECTRICAL RESISTANCE
2.	LUMENS	B.	DISTANCE IN SPACE
3.	HECTARES	C.	HEAT
4.	PECKS	D.	AIR PRESSURE
5.	KNOTS	E.	HARDNESS
6.	ANGSTROM UNITS	F.	OLDEN LINEAR MEASURE
7.	SQUARE FEET	G.	LOUDNESS OF SOUND
8.	REAMS	H.	WEIGHT OF GEMS
9.	B.T.U.'S	I.	HORSE RACE COURSE
10.	EMS	J.	BOOZE
11.	OHMS	K.	DEPTH OF WATER
12.	FURLONGS	L.	EARTHQUAKES
13.	MACH NUMBERS	M.	EARTHS AGES
14.	DECIBELS	N.	WATER BEHIND A DAM
15.	CUBITS	O.	LENGTH OF LIGHTWAVES
16.	HANDS	P.	SPEED ON/IN WATER
17.	ACRE FEET	Q.	HEAT OF PEPPERS
18.	PARSECS	R.	WIND SPEED
19.	INCHES OF Hg	S.	SPEED IN AIR
20.	ON THE MOHS SCALE	T.	QUANTITY OF PAPER
21.	CARATS	U.	HORSE HEIGHT
22.	GILL	V.	LAND
23.	ON RICHTER SCALE	W.	TYPE FONTS
24.	EPOCHS	X.	PRODUCE
25.	BEAUFORT SCALE	Y.	HOUSING FLOOR PLAN
26.	SCOVILLE UNITS	Z.	FLOW OF LIGHT

PHOBIAS (REAL AND IMAGINED)

1.	ACOUSTICOPHOBIA	A.	THE DEAD
2.	ACROPHOBIA	B.	SUNLIGHT
3.	AGORAHOBIA	C.	ONESELF
4.	ANGLOPHOBIA	D.	FLYING
5.	ARACHNOPHOBIA	E.	NOISES
6.	AUTOPHOBIA	F.	STEALING
7.	AVIOPHOBIA	G.	THINGS ENGLISH
8.	BIBLIOPHOBIA	H.	WATER
9.	CARCINOPHOBIA	I.	SLEEP
10.	CLAUSTROPHOBIA	J.	FIRE
11.	FRANCOPHOBIA	K.	SPIDERS
12.	GYMNOPHOBIA	L.	PLEASURE
13.	GYNOPHOBIA	M.	NUMBER 13
14.	HEDONOPHOBIA	N.	GOD
15.	HELIOPHOBIA	O.	THINGS FRENCH
16.	HEMOPHOBIA	P.	CONFINED SPACE
17.	HERPAPHOBIA	Q.	FOREIGNERS
18.	HYDROPHOBIA	R.	CANCER
19.	KLEPTOPHOBIA	S.	HEIGHTS
20.	NECROPHOBIA	T.	BOOKS
21.	PHOBOPHOBIA	U.	NUDITY
22.	PYROPHOBIA	V.	SNAKES
23.	SOMNIPHOBIA	W.	OPEN SPACES
24.	THEOPHOBIA	X.	BLOOD
25.	TRISKAIDEKAPHOBIA	Y.	WOMEN
26.	XENOPHOBIA	Z.	FEAR

DEM BONES

1. KNEE CAPE
2. FUNNY BONE
3. THE EAR'S STIRRUP
4. SHINBONE
5. LONGEST NERVE
6. COLLARBONE
7. MAIN ARTERY FROM HEART
8. BREASTBONE
9. VEIN TO THE HEART
10. TAILBONE
11. TOES
12. WRIST BONES
13. LARGE FOREARM BONE
14. JAWBONE
15. THE LONGEST BONE

A. STAPES
B. MANDIBLE
C. CLAVICLE
D. STERNUM
E. AORTA
F. VENA CAVA
G. HUMERUS
H. ULNA
I. SCIATIC
J. CARPALS
K. COCCYX
L. FEMUR
M. PATELLA
N. TIBIA
O. PHALANGES

PILLS FOR EVERY PURPOSE

1.	LIPITOR		A.	IMPOTENCE
2.	PRILOSEC		B.	ANGINA
3.	GLUCOPHAGE		C.	SINUS CONGESTION
4.	AMOXICILLIN		D.	HAIR LOSS
5.	CLARITIN		E.	ATTENTION DEFICIT
6.	PROZAC		F.	ASTHMA
7.	IBUPROFEN		G.	HYPERTENSION
8.	ORTHO-NOVUM		H.	ALLERGY, SEASONAL
9.	ZYRTEC		I.	PSYCHOSIS
10.	VIAGRA		J.	HIGH CHOLESTEROL
11.	DIAZEPAN		K.	INFECTION
12.	VALIUM		L.	FLATULENCE
13.	NASONEX		M.	DIABETES
14.	VASOTEC		N.	MALARIA
15.	NITRO GLYCERIN		O.	ULCERS
16.	TAXOL		P.	ANXIETY
17.	ANBESOL		Q.	CONGESTIVE HEART FAILURE
18.	QUININE		R.	PAIN, GENERAL
19.	RITALIN		S.	PAIN, DENTAL
20.	ALBUTEROL		T.	DEPRESSION
21.	ROGAIN		U.	ALLERGY, PERENNIAL
22.	RISPERDAL		V.	BREAST CANCER
23.	DIGOXIN		W.	CONTRACEPTION
24.	PHAZYME		X.	EPILEPSY

THE SCHOOLS OF THE NCAA

1.	BRINGHAM YOUNG	A.	MALIBU, CA
2.	BALL STATE.	B.	ANNAPOLIS, MD
3.	BAYLOR U	C.	NASHVILLE, TN
4.	BUCKNELL U	D.	BUFFALO, NY
5.	CANISIUS	E.	PHILA, PA
6.	COLGATE	F.	LEWISBURG, PA
7.	CORNELL	G.	PITTSBURGH, PA
8.	THE CITADEL	H.	DURHAM, NC
9.	DARTMOUTH	I.	SPOKANE, WA
10.	DEPAUL U	J.	HEMPSTEAD, NY
11.	DREXEL U	K.	NORFOLK, VA
12.	DUKE U	L.	BETHLEHEM, PA
13.	DUQUESNE U	M.	TULSA, OK
14.	FORDHAM U	N.	HANOVER, NH
15.	GEORGETOWN	O.	CHICAGO, IL
16.	GONZAGA	P.	WINSTON SALEM, NC
17.	HOFSTRA U	Q.	ITHACA, NY
18.	LEHIGH U	R.	MUNCIE, IN
19.	LOYOLA MARYMOUNT	S.	WACO, TX
20.	OLD DOMINION	T.	PROVO, UT
21.	ORAL ROBERTS U	U.	WASHINGTON, DC
22.	PEPPERDINE U	V.	CHARLESTON, SC
23.	US NAVAL ACADEMY	W.	WEST POINT, NY
24.	US MILITARY ACADEMY	X.	BRONX, NY
25.	VANDERBILT U	Y.	LOS ANGELES, CA
26.	WAKE FOREST	Z.	HAMILTON, NY

WORDS FROM A TO Z

1.	ANTHRACITE	A.	PERIOD OF REST
2.	BOUYANT	B.	A DOCK OR WHARF
3.	CHRISM	C.	HATRED OF FOREIGNERS
4.	DUCTILE	D.	TYPE OR PART OF SOIL
5.	EGRESS	E.	HARD COAL
6.	FECUND	F.	A SHORT ROPE
7.	GUILE	G.	ABOMINABLE SNOWMAN
8.	HUMUS	H.	ABILITY TO FLOAT
9.	INGENUE	I.	WOMANS HEAD COVERING
10.	JETSAM	J.	NOT BRITTLE
11.	KLEZMER	K.	HAVING TO DO WITH THE SEA
12.	LANYARD	L.	TO FEEL REMORSE
13.	MUTATE	M.	FERTILE
14.	NAUTICAL	N.	THE CHEST AREA
15.	OLIGARCHY	O.	CAJUN STYLE MUSIC
16.	PICAYUNE	P.	A TYPE OF JEWISH MUSIC
17.	QUAY	Q.	AN EXIT
18.	RUE	R.	CUNNING
19.	SABATICAL	S.	RULE BY A FEW
20.	THORAX	T.	INNOCENT YOUNG GIRL
21.	UNGULATE	U.	TO CHANGE
22.	VERACITY	V.	SACRAMENTAL OIL
23.	WIMPLE	W.	A MAMMAL WITH HOOFS
24.	XENOPHOBIA	X.	PETTY OR TRIVIAL
25.	YETI	Y.	HONESTY/TRUTHFULNESS
26.	ZYDECO	Z.	DISCHARGED FROM A SHIP

TV THEME SONGS

1.	ALL IN THE FAMILY	A.	LIGHT THE LIGHTS
2.	ADDAMS FAMILY	B.	WHEN HE WAS ONLY 3
3.	BEVERLY HILLBILLIES	C.	CAN'T DO THE TIME
4.	PATTY DUKE SHOW	D.	LIKE H. HOOVER AGAIN
5.	GILLIGAN'S ISLAND	E.	SATIN TIGHTS
6.	MR. ED	F.	SOMETIMES YOU WANT
7.	THE JEFFERSONS	G.	A BUBBLIN CRUDE
8.	WKRP IN CINCINNATI	H.	SCRAMBLED EGGS
9.	CHEERS	I.	STUCK IN SECOND GEAR
10.	WONDER YEARS	J.	COULD YOU BE MINE
11.	FRASIER	K.	SOME FLY BY DAY
12.	FRESH PRINCE	L.	ALL TOGETHER OOKY
13.	FRIENDS	M.	PACKING & UNPACKING
14.	MARRIED WITH CHILDREN	N.	WHAT A CRAZY PAIR
15.	SUDDENLY, SUSAN	O.	IN WEST PHILADELPHIA
16.	BARETTA	P.	I'M GONNA LEARN TO FLY
17.	MOONLIGHTING	Q.	KEEP SMILIN UNTIL THEN
18.	WONDER WOMAN	R.	A PIECE OF THE PIE
19.	THE MUPPET SHOW	S.	LEND ME YOUR EARS
20.	DAVY CROCKETT	T.	I'M STRONG TO THE FINISH
21.	ROY ROGERS	U.	HORSE & CARRIAGE
22.	FAME	V.	OF COURSE, OF COURSE
23.	MR. ROGERS	W.	THERE AIN'T MUCH HOPE
24.	POPEYE	X.	A THREE HOUR TOUR
25.	ANDY GRIFFITH SHOW	Y.	HE'S GOTTA FIGHT WITH ME
26.	BONANZA	Z.	AT THE FISHIN HOLE

I WAS FIRST

1.	BREAK SOUND BARRIER (M)	A.	CHRISTAAN BARNARD
2.	PITCH A PERFECT GAME (1904)	B.	CHARLES LINDBURGH
3.	CLIMB MOUNT EVEREST	C.	CLARENCE BIRDSEYE
4.	FIRST MOVIE TARAZAN (DISP)	D.	ELIZABETH A SETON
5.	FLY ACROSS ATLANTIC SOLO	E.	CHUCK YEAGER
6.	FIRST WOMAN IN SPACE	F.	VIRGINIA DARE
7.	FIRST HEART TRANSPLANT	G.	ELMO LINCOLN
8.	BREAK SOUND BARRIER (F)	H.	NEIL ARMSTRONG
9.	PILOT FIRST FLIGHT (PLANE)	I.	ELIZ. BLACKWELL
10.	STEP ON THE MOON	J.	MIKE MORRISON
11.	BREAK 4 MINUTE MILE	K.	ROBERT FULTON
12.	DIE IN ELECTRIC CHAIR	L.	JACQUELINE COCHRAN
13.	EXCEED 600 MPH IN A CAR	M.	FRANK ZAMBONI
14.	SWIM ENGLISH CHANNEL (F)	N.	STEVEN JOBS
15.	FIRST WOMAN IN THE NHL	O.	THOMAS EDISON
16.	FIRST MAN IN SPACE	P.	CRAIG BREEDLOVE
17.	AMERICAN WOMAN MD	Q.	EDWIN LAND
18.	SOLD FROZEN FOOD	R.	YURI GAGARIN
19.	BUILT FIRST PC	S.	EDMUND HILLARY
20.	BUILT 1ST STEAMBOAT	T.	ELISHA OTIS
21.	1ST 'INSTANT' CAMERA	U.	ROGER BANNISTER
22.	1ST USEFUL ELEVATOR	V.	ORVILLE WRIGHT
23.	ICE RESURFACER	W.	GERTRUDE EDERLY
24.	PHONOGRAPH MACHINE	X.	MANON RHEAUME
25.	1ST AMERICAN SAINT	Y.	VALENTINA TERESHKOVA
26.	FIRST CHILD BORN IN AMERICAN OF EUROPEAN PARENTS	Z.	WILLIAM KEMMLER

WEIRD TOOLS

1.	BRACE AND BIT	A.	WHERE A LAB GROWS MICROORGANISMS
2.	ENTERENCHING TOOL	B.	TYPE OF SUITCASE
3.	CLAVICLE BOARD	C.	GUITAR PICK
4.	FIFTH WHEEL	D.	A GRINDING(CRUSHING) TOOL
5.	HEMOSTAT	E.	STERILIZING MACHINE
6.	HAWSER	F.	MAESTRO'S STICK
7.	CHURCH KEY	G.	A SHIPS PRECISE NAVIGATION CLOCK
8.	ABACUS	H.	A HAND DRILL
9.	BOLA	I.	DOUBLE REED HORN
10.	EPEE	J.	JOINS TRACTOR & TRAILER
11.	TRANSIT	K.	COMPUTER STORAGE DEVICE
12.	AUTOCLAVE	L.	SURGICAL CLAMP
13.	PLECTRUM	M.	LIFE BOAT LOWERING DEVICE
14.	OBOE	N.	A SOLDIER'S SHOVEL
15.	VALISE	O.	KEY HOLDER
16.	PESTLE	P.	MEASURES MILES DRIVEN
17.	SPANNER	Q.	BOTTLE OPENER
18.	ZIP DRIVE	R.	AN IRISHMANS' CLUB
19.	GIMBALED CHRONOMETER	S.	A PILOT'S ATTITUDE INDICATOR
20.	PETRI DISH	T.	CROSSMEMBER OVER A DOOR
21.	BATON	U.	FENCING SWORD
22.	ARTIFICAL HORIZON	V.	FIREMAN'S HOSE WRENCH
23.	LINTEL	W.	SURVEYORS TELESCOPE
24.	DAVIT	X.	LARGE ROPE USED ON SHIPS
25.	ODOMETER	Y.	ORIENTAL COUTNING DEVICE
26.	SHILLELAGH	Z.	GAUCHO'S THROWING WEAPON

WHERE AM I?

1.	AREA 51	A.	NEW ZEALAND
2.	KHYBER PASS	B.	VIETNAM
3.	SEA OF TRANQUILLITY	C.	WASHINGTON
4.	THE GRAND CANYON	D.	HAWAII
5.	LOCH NESS	E.	PHILIPPINES
6.	NAPA VALLEY	F.	SPAIN
7.	GOLAN HEIGHTS	G.	AFGHANISTAN
8.	BAY OF PIGS	H.	NEVADA
9.	BLACK FOREST	I.	NORWAY
10.	MEKONG DELTA	J.	UTAH
11.	LAKE OKEECHOBEE	K.	HONG KONG
12.	THE ALHAMBRA	L.	INDIA
13.	THE PAMPAS	M.	GERMANY
14.	DIAMOND HEAD	N.	CALIFORNIA
15.	THE GINZA	O.	CUBA
16.	THE NILE DELTA	P.	SCOTLAND
17.	GREAT SALT LAKE	Q.	MEXICO
18.	THE GRAND BANKS	R.	THE MOON
19.	NORTH ISLAND	S.	EGYPT
20.	THE GREAT FJORDS	T.	ISRAEL
21.	KOWLOON	U.	ARIZONA
22.	CORREGIDOR	V.	JAPAN
23.	BIG BEN	W.	ARGENTINA
24.	TAJ MAHAL	X.	FLORIDA
25.	PUGET SUOND	Y.	CANADA
26.	CHICHEN ITZA	Z.	ENGLAND

MIDDLE NAMES

1.	ALVA	A.	HUBERT HUMPHREY
2.	BIRCHARD	B.	JAMES PENNEY
3.	CASH	C.	JOHN KENNEDY
4.	DELANO	D.	EDGAR BURROUGHS
5.	EARL	E.	RICHARD NIXON
6.	FITZGERALD	F.	JOHN MORGAN
7.	GAMALIEL	G.	THOMAS EDISON
8.	HORATIO	H.	FRANKLIN ROOSEVELT
9.	ILLICH	I.	BERNARD MONTGOMERY
10.	JAMES	J.	JOHN GARNER
11.	KING	K.	WILLIAM SHERMAN
12.	LAW	L.	WARREN HARDING
13.	MILHOUS	M.	JOHN ADAMS
14.	NANCE	N.	MILTON HERSHEY
15.	ORVILLE	O.	OLIVER HOLMES
16.	PIERPONT	P.	JAMES (JIMMY) CARTER
17.	QUINCY	Q.	FRANK FELLER
18.	RICE	R.	EUGENE DEBS
19.	SNAVLEY	S.	RUTHERFORD HAYES
20.	TECUMSHA	T.	NAT COLE
21.	VICTOR	V.	JOHN AUDUBON
22.	WENDELL	W.	WILLIAM DOUGLAS
23.	XAVIER	X.	VLADIMIR LENNIN

ADS WE ALL KNOW

1. YOU DESERVE A BREAK TODAY
2. _____ TASTES GOOD LIKE A _____ SHOULD.
3. THINGS GO BETTER WITH _____
4. ONLY _____ _____ KNOWS FOR SURE
5. SOMETHING SPECIAL IN THE _____.
6. I'D WALK A MILE FOR A _____.
7. TAKES A LICKING & KEEPS ON TICKING.
8. HOME OF THE WHOPPER

9. MADE FROM THE BEST STUFF ON EARTH
10. WE TRY HARDER
11. I'D RATHER FIGHT THAN SWITCH.
12. SEE THE U.S.A. IN YOUR
13. TIME WELL SPENT
14. LET _____ TAKE YOU HOME
15. YOU'RE IN GOOD HANDS WITH _____
16. 99 AND 44/100% PURE
17. WE NEVER SLEEP.
18. THE COMPANY YOU KEEP
19. DON'T LEAVE HOME WITHOUT IT
20. WHEN IT RAINS, IT POURS
21. A LITTLE DAB WILL DO YA
22. WE BRING GOOD THINGS TO LIFE
23. NOBODY DOESN'T LIKE _____
24. GOOD TO THE LAST DROP
25. ITS BETTER IN THE

26. I CAN'T BELIEVE I ATE THE WHOLE THING

A. COKE
B. MCDONALDS
C. NEW YORK LIFE
D. CHEVROLET
E. SARA LEE
F. ATLAS (VAN LINES)
G. LADY CLAIROL
H. PINKERTON DETECTIVES
I. BRYCLCREME
J. G.E.
K. ALKA SELTZER
L. AMERICAN EXPRESS
M. BURGER KING
N. WINSTON
O. MORTON SALT
P. A & E CHANNEL
Q. BAHAMAS
R. SNAPPLE
S. CAMEL
T. IVORY SOAP
U. TARRYTON
V. MAXWELL HOUSE
W. AVIS
X. TIMEX
Y. ALLSTATE INSURANCE
Z. AMERICAN AIRLINES

MORE ADS

1.	MMM GOOD	A.	NIKE
2.	HAVE IT YOUR WAY	B.	NEW YORK
3.	YOU'RE GETTIN A—DUDE	C.	VISA CARD
4.	SOMETIMES YOU FEEL LIKE A NUT	D.	CHARMIN
5.	SOMETIME YOU DON'T	E.	BURGER KING
6.	BREAKFAST OF CHAMPIONS	F.	ARPEGE PERFUME
7.	NO MORE TEARS	G.	OSCAR MEYER WIENERS
8.	I'M WORTH IT	H.	TACO BELL
9.	DIAMONDS ARE FOREVER	I.	MOUNDS
10.	I LOVE	J.	DELL COMPUTER
11.	_____ SEEDS GROW	K.	CAMPBELL SOUP
12.	GOT _____	L.	NOXEMA
13.	I WISH I WERE AN	M.	QUAKER PUFFED WHEAT
14.	WE ANSWER TO A HIGHER AUTHORITY	N.	J & J BABY SHAMPOO
15.	FINGER LICKIN GOOD	O.	ROLAIDS
16.	HEAD FOR THE MOUNTAINS	P.	MILK
17.	HEAD FOR THE BORDER	Q.	WHEATIES
18.	DON'T SQUEEZE THE	R.	COKE
19.	JUST DO IT	S.	DE BEERS
20.	MELTS IN YOUR MOUTH	T.	ALMOND JOY
21.	HOW DO YOU SPELL RELIEF	U.	KFC
22.	IT'S SHOT FROM GUNS	V.	BUSCH BEER
23.	PROMISE HER ANYTHING	W.	HEBREW NAT'L HOT DOGS
24.	EVERYWHERE U WANT TO BE	X.	M & M'S
25.	IT'S THE REAL THING	Y.	BURPEE
26.	TAKE IT OFF TAKE IT ALL OFF	Z.	PREFERENCE BY L'OREAL

PRE PRESIDENTIAL JOBS

1. PEANUT FARMER
2. TAILOR
3. MINING ENGINEER
4. COLLEGE PRESIDENT
5. CHIEF JUSTICE OF THE U.S. (AFTER PRES)
6. LABOR UNION LEADER
7. PRINTER (NEWSPAPER OWNER)
8. HABERDASHER
9. LEATHER MAKER
10. ASST. FOOTBALL COACH
11. POSTMASTER
12. CIA DIRECTOR
13. LAND SURVEYOR
14. ASST. SECRETARY OF THE NAVY
15. MINISTER TO RUSSIA (& A BACHELOR)
16. SMALL COMBAT BOAT CAPTAIN
17. CATTLE RANCHER
18. FIVE STAR GENERAL
19. TEACHER (PUBLIC SPEAKING)
20. CANAL BOATMAN (NY)
21. SON OF A U.S. PRESIDENT
22. U.S. PRESIDENT (NON CONSECUTIVE)
23. FARMER, INVENTOR, SCIENTIST, LINGUIST, ARICHITECT, PHILOSOPER, ETC, ETC, ETC.

A. U.S. GRANT
B. HERBERT HOOVER
C. J. F. KENNEDY
D. D. D. EISENHOWER

E. HARRY TRUMAN
F. JIMMY CARTER
G. GROVER CLEVELAND
H. ANDREW JOHNSON
I. JAMES A. GARFIELD
J. W.H. TAFT
K. RONALD REAGAN
L. T. ROOSEVELT
M. L.B. JOHNSON
N. GEORGE BUSH

O. F.D. ROOSEVELT
P. WARREN G. HARDING
Q. GERALD FORD
R. THOMAS JEFFERSON
S. JOHN Q. ADAMS
T. ABE LINCOLN
U. GEORGE WASHINGTON

V. JAMES BUCHANAN

W. WOODROW WILSON

ALPHABET SOUP

1.	CHARLES, PRINCE OF WALES	A.	HRH
2.	YOUR CAR CLUB	B.	AAA
3.	FEDERAL TAX AGCY.	C.	IRS
4.	THE SHOOTING SPORTS	D.	NRA
5.	BROADCASTING LICENSES	E.	FCC
6.	PLANE CRASHES	F.	NTSB
7.	JOB SAFETY	G.	OSHA
8.	CROOKED STOCKBROKERS	H.	SEC
9.	PARCEL POST	I.	USPS
10.	DEADLY DISEASE	J.	CDC
11.	THE NATIONAL BUDGET	K.	OMB
12.	A KIDNAPPING	L.	FBI
13.	AUTO RACING	M.	NASCAR
14.	A DOG'S PEDIGREE	N.	AKC
15.	QUALITY OF MEAT	O.	USDA
16.	PRESCRIPTION MEDICATIONS	P.	FDA
17.	FOLLOWS A LAWYERS NAME	Q.	ESQ
18.	LET'S FORM A UNION	R.	NLRB
19.	INSPECTS BIG RIGS	S.	DOT
20.	SINGING 4 PART HARMONY	T.	SPEBSQSA
21.	A UNION SEAMSTRESS	U.	ILGWU
22.	THE MORMONS	V.	LDS
23.	ROOT CANAL DOCTOR	W.	DDS
24.	A SOCIAL SERVICE CLUB	X.	BPOE
25.	A SCHOOL ORGANIZATION	Y.	PTA
26.	SHOTS BEFORE YOU TRAVEL	Z.	WHO

ANIMALS ETC.

1.	MANX	A.	A TAILLESS CAT
2.	CLYDESDALE	B.	A DRAFT HORSE
3.	CAIMAN	C.	LIKE A SMALL ALLIGATOR
4.	HEIFER	D.	A COW THAT NEVER CALVED
5.	KODIAK	E.	A VERY LARGE BEAR
6.	HAMMERHEAD	F.	A TYPE OF SHARK
7.	PEREGRINE	G.	A KIND OF FALCON
8.	SNOWSHOE	H.	A NORTH AMERICAN RABBIT
9.	ANGORA	I.	A FINE HAIRED GOAT
10.	MUTTON	J.	OBTAINED FROM SHEEP
11.	DUCKBILL	K.	A PLATYPUS
12.	BACTRIAN	L.	A TWO HUMPED CAMEL
13.	WALLABY	M.	LIKE A SMALL KANGAROO
14.	SIDEWINDER	N.	A TYPE OF RATTLESNAKE
15.	NUTRIA	O.	A WATER RODENT
16.	VICUNA	P.	A SMALL LLAMA
17.	DINGO	Q.	AUSTRALIAN WILD DOG
18.	JERABOA	R.	AN ASIAN RODENT
19.	MAN O' WAR	S.	A TYPE OF JELLYFISH
20.	WAPITI	T.	A REINDEER (ETC)
21.	BENGAL	U.	A TYPE OF TIGER
22.	ALSATIAN	V.	A DOMESTIC DOG (USED BY THE BRITISH)
23.	POLECAT	W.	A NICKNAME FOR A SKUNK
24.	EMPEROR	X.	A TYPE OF PENGUIN
25.	CYGNET	Y.	A BABY SWAN
26.	BROWN RECLUSE	Z.	A POISONOUS SPIDER

ANIMAL WORDS

1.	ARACHNID	A.	SPIDER
2.	SERPENTINE	B.	SNAKE LIKE
3.	TERRAPIN	C.	TURTLE TYPE
4.	WAPITI	D.	REINDEER
5.	URSINE	E.	BEAR LIKE
6.	MONARCH	F.	A BUTTERFLY TYPE
7.	QUAHOG	G.	TYPE OF CLAM
8.	PORCINE	H.	PIG LIKE
9.	CASSOWARY	I.	A LARGE BIRD
10.	WILDEBEEST	J.	A TYPE OF GNU
11.	GANDER	K.	A MALE GOOSE
12.	CANINE	L.	DOG LIKE
13.	KATYDID	M.	A NOISY INSECT
14.	WALLABY	N.	LIKE A KANGAROO
15.	PORTUGUESE MAN O WAR	O.	TYPE OF JELLYFISH
16.	YAK	P.	AN OX FROM TIBET
17.	BALEEN	Q.	A TYPE OF WHALE
18.	FELINE	R.	CAT LIKE
19.	MUSKELLUNGE	S.	A GAME FISH
20.	GILA MONSTER	T.	POISONOUS LIZARD
21.	DRONE	U.	A MALE BEE
22.	PRAWN	V.	A LARGE SHRIMP
23.	BOVINE	W.	COW LIKE
24.	DRAKE	X.	A MALE DUCK
25.	PTERODACTYL	Y.	FLYING DINOSAUR
26.	ALPACA	Z.	TYPE OF LLAMA

ANIMALS IN FACT & FICTION

1.	TRIGGER	A.	ROY ROGERS
2.	CHECKERS	B.	RICHARD NIXON
3.	OLD BO	C.	ROOSTER COGBURN
4.	FRED	D.	BARETTA
5.	ASTRO	E.	THE JETSONS
6.	LITTLE BLACKIE	F.	MATTI ROSS (TRUE GRIT)
7.	LASSIE	G.	TIMMY
8.	BUTTERMILK	H.	DALE EVANS
9.	EDDIE	I.	MARTIN CRANE
10.	SOCKS	J.	BILL CLINTON
11.	CUFF & LINK	K.	ROCKY BALBOA
12.	FALA	L.	FDR
13.	SILVER	M.	THE LONE RANGER
14.	BOBBY (GREYFRIERS)	N.	AULD JACK
15.	ASTA	O.	THE THIN MAN
16.	MILLIE	P.	BARBARA BUSH
17.	BUCEPHALUS	Q.	ALEXANDER THE GREAT
18.	SCOOBY DO	R.	SHAGGY
19.	PETEY (PETE THE PUP)	S.	OUR GANG
20.	WHITE FANG	T.	GREY BEAVER
21.	MR. ED	U.	WILBUR POST
22.	RIN TIN TIN	V.	RUSTY
23.	RIKKI TIKKI TAVI	W.	TEDDY
24.	CHARLEY	X.	JOHN STEINBECK
25.	TRAVELLER	Y.	ROBERT E. LEE
26.	FRANCIS THE TALKING MULE	Z.	PETE STERLING

WHEN I GROW UP I WANT TO BE A

1.	ANTLING	A.	ANT
2.	KIT	B.	FOX
3.	PUSSY	C.	CAT
4.	NESTLING	D.	BIRD (EX: FALCON)
5.	SPIKE BULL	E.	BUFFALO
6.	SMOLTS	F.	SALMON
7.	KID	G.	GOAT
8.	TADPOLE	H.	FROG
9.	SHOAT	I.	PIG
10.	BUNNY	J.	RABBIT
11.	WHELP	K.	DOG
12.	POULT	L.	CHICKEN
13.	ELVER	M.	EEL
14.	FOAL	N.	HORSE
15.	SQUAB	O.	PIGEON
16.	SPAWN	P.	FISH (EX: TROUT)
17.	JOEY	Q.	KANGAROO
18.	HOWLET	R.	OWL
19.	LITTLENECK	S.	CLAM
20.	CYGNET	T.	SWAN
21.	LAMB	U.	SHEEP
22.	BACHELOR	V.	SEAL
23.	CUB	W.	BEAR
24.	DRAY	X.	SQUIRREL
25.	FAWN	Y.	DEER
26.	GOSLING	Z.	GOOSE

MAKES AND MODELS

1.	AMIGO	A.	ISUZU
2.	APOLLO	B.	BUICK
3.	AURORA	C.	OLDSMOBILE
4.	CIMARRON	D.	CADILLAC
5.	COMANCHE	E.	JEEP
6.	CORDOBA	F.	CHRYSLER
7.	COSMOPOLITAN	G.	LINCOLN
8.	CRESSIDA	H.	TOYOTA
9.	DAYTONA SPYDER	I.	FERRARI
10.	DELSOL	J.	HONDA
11.	DIPLOMAT	K.	DODGE
12.	ESPADA	L.	LAMBORGHINI
13.	FAIRLANE	M.	FORD
14.	FOX	N.	AUDI
15.	FUEGO	O.	RENAULT
16.	JAVELIN	P.	AMC
17.	LEMANS	Q.	PONTIAC
18.	MILLENIA	R.	MAZDA
19.	MONZA	S.	CHEVROLET
20.	PULSAR	T.	NISSAN
21.	SCIROCCO	U.	VOLKSWAGEN
22.	SIERRA	V.	GMC TRUCK
23.	STARION	W.	MITSUBISHI
24.	TIBURON	X.	HYUNDAI
25.	VOLARE	Y.	PLYMOUTH
26.	ZEPHER	Z.	MERCURY

Thanks to Paul and Caesar

FROM THE BIBLE

1.	NOAH	A.	BUILT THE ARC
2.	JOB	B.	KNOWN FOR GREAT PATIENCE
3.	LOT	C.	HIS WIFE TURNED TO SALT
4.	DELILAH	D.	TEMPTED SAMPSON
5.	SOLOMON	E.	KNOWN FOR HIS WISDOM
6.	MELCHIOR	F.	KNOWS GASPAR & BALTHASAR
7.	AARON	G.	OLDER BROTHER OF MOSES
8.	DAVID	H.	SLEW THE GIANT
9.	GABRIEL	I.	AN ARCHANGEL
10.	JOSHUA	J.	FOUGHT AT JERICO
11.	DANIEL	K.	FACED THE LIONS IN THEIR DENS
12.	ISSAC	L.	SON OF ABRAHAM
13.	ABEDNEGO	M.	FRIENDS, SHADRACH & MESHACH
14.	CAIN	N.	OLDER BROTHER OF ABEL
15.	ELIZABETH	O.	MOTHER OF JOHN THE BAPTIST
16.	CAIAPHAS	P.	CHARGED JESUS WITH BLASPHEMY
17.	RUTH	Q.	GREAT GRANDMOTHER OF DAVID
18.	METHUSELAH	R.	LIVED TO AGE 969
19.	ELISHA	S.	SUCCESSOR TO ELIJAH
20.	SAUL	T.	FIRST KING OF ISRAEL
21.	SALOME	U.	DANCED FOR JOHNS HEAD
22.	LAZARUS	V.	RAISED FROM THE DEAD
23.	ESTHER	W.	BECAME QUEEN OF PERSIA
24.	JONAH	X.	SWALLOWED BY A WHALE
25.	THOMAS	Y.	FULL OF DOUBT
26.	MELCHISEDECH	Z.	AN EARLY JUDAIC PRIEST

PATRON SAINTS

1.	BATTLE	A.	ARCHANGEL MICHAEL
2.	BREWERS	B.	WENCESLAUS
3.	CARPENTERS	C.	JOSEPH
4.	CATHOLIC CHARITIES	D.	VINCENT DE PAUL
5.	CEMETERY KEEPERS	E.	JOSEPH OF ARIMATHEA
6.	MOTHERS	F.	ANNE
7.	CIVIL SERVANTS.	G.	THOMAS MOORE
8.	COLLEGES	H.	THOMAS AQUINAS
9.	DANCERS	I.	VITUS
10.	ENGLAND	J.	GEORGE
11.	FISHERMAN	K.	PETER
12.	FLORISTS	L.	ROSE OF LIMA
13.	FRANCE	M.	JOAN OF ARC
14.	IRELAND	N.	PATRICK
15.	ITALY	O.	FRANCIS OF ASSISI
16.	JOURNEYS	P.	CHRISTOPHER
17.	LOST CAUSES	Q.	JUDE
18.	LOVERS	R.	VALENTINE
19.	PHARMACISTS	S.	COSMOS AND DAMIEN
20.	POLAND	T.	STANISLAUS
21.	RUSSIA	U.	BASIL THE GREAT
22.	SCOTLAND	V.	ANDREW
23.	SEMINARIANS	W.	CHARLES BORROMEO
24.	THIEVES (GOOD ONES ??)	X.	DISMAS
25.	THROAT AILMENTS	Y.	BLAISE
26.	VENICE	Z.	MARK

A VERY CATHOLIC VOCABULARY

1.	ABSOLUTION	A.	REMISSION OF SINS
2.	ALB	B.	A WHITE LINEN VESTMENT
3.	BETHROTHAL	C.	A PROMISE OF MARRIAGE
4.	BEATIFIED	D.	STEP TOWARD SAINTOOD
5.	CANA	E.	SITE OF CHRIST'S FIRST MIRACLE
6.	CASSOCK	F.	A PRIESTS 33 BUTTON VESTMENT
7.	EX CATHEDRA	G.	FROM THE BISHOPS CHAIR
8.	DOGMA	H.	A TRUTH OF FAITH OR MORALS
9.	ENCYCLICAL	I.	POPES LETTER ABOUT FAITH
10.	EXORCISM	J.	RITUAL TO DRIVE OUT DEMONS
11.	EXTREME UNCTION	K.	THE LAST RITES OF THE CHURCH
12.	GETHSEMANI	L.	GARDEN OF CHRIST'S ARREST
13.	GOLGOTHA	M.	WHERE CHRIST WAS CRUCFIED
14.	HOMILY	N.	THE SERMON AFTER THE GOSPEL
15.	HOSANNA	O.	WORD SPOKEN OR SUNG IN PRAISE
16.	INQUISITION	P.	COURT INVESTIGATING HERESY
17.	GENUFLEXION	Q.	BENDING 1 KNEE TO THE GROUND
18.	KYRIE ELEISON	R.	GREEK FOR LORD HAVE MERCY
19.	MAGNIFICAT	S.	A PRAYER TO OUR LADY
20.	MITRE	T.	A BISHOP'S HAT
21.	ETCUM SPIRITU TUO	U.	AND WITH THY SPIRIT
22.	PATER NOSTER	V.	OUR FATHER
23.	CONFIETOR DEO	W.	I CONFESS TO GOD
24.	DOMINUS VOBISCUM	X.	THE LORD BE WITH YOU
25.	OREMUS	Y.	LET US PRAY
26.	PAX DOMINI	Z.	THE PEACE OF THE LORD

A VERY JEWISH VOCABULARY

WITH A LITTLE YIDDISH THROWN IN

1.	BABUSHKA	A.	A KERCHIEF AS A HEAD COVERING
2.	BAT/BAR MITZVA	B.	A GIRL/BOY COMING OF AGE CEREMONY
3.	BUBBY	C.	A GRANDMOTHER
4.	BUPKES	D.	SOMETHING WORTHLESS
5.	CHUTZPAH	E.	NERVE OR GALL
6.	DREIDEL	F.	TOY TOP USED AT CHANUKAH
7.	GELT	G.	MONEY (ESP. GIVEN AT CHANUKAH)
8.	HORA	H.	A FESTIVE CIRCLE DANCE
9.	KADDISH	I.	TRADITIONAL PRAYER OF MOURNING
10.	KIBBUTZ	J.	AN ISRAELI COLLECTIVE FARM
11.	KLEZMER	K.	A STYLE OF MUSIC
12.	KNESSET	L.	THE ISRAELI PARLIAMENT
13.	LIKUD	M.	ISRAEL'S CONSERVATIVE PARTY
14.	L'CHAIM	N.	A TOAST, MEANING "TO LIFE"
15.	MAZEL TOV	O.	A PHRASE OF CONGRATULATIONS
16.	MENSCH	P.	A GOOD GUY OR REAL MAN
17.	MESHUGENE	Q.	A CRAZY PERSON
18.	NOSH	R.	A OR TO SNACK
19.	OY VEY	S.	OH NO (PHRASE OF GRIEF OR PAIN)
20.	SCHLEP	T.	TO CARRY A LOAD
21.	SEDER	U.	A CEREMONIAL MEAL
22.	SHABBAT	V.	THE SABBATH DAY
23.	SHALOM	W.	PEACE (USED AS A GREETING)
24.	SHOAH	X.	THE HOLOCAUST
25.	SHOFAR	Y.	MUSICAL INST. MADE FROM A RAMS HORN
26.	YARMULKE	Z.	A SKULL CAP

I'M SO HUNGRY I COULD EAT A HORSE

IF I KNEW WHICH OF THESE WAS A HORSE

1.	ESCARGOT	A.	SNAILS
2.	COQ A VAN	B.	CHICKEN IN WINE
3.	COQUILLE ST JAQUES	C.	SCALLOPS/POTATOES/MUSH ROOMS/CHEESE
4.	L'OUEF	D.	EGGS
5.	BORSCHT	E.	BEET SOUP
6.	BANGERS & MASH	F.	SAUSAGE & MASHED POTATOES
7.	LE GLAZE	G.	ICE CREAM
8.	POLLOS CON ARROZ	H.	CHICKEN WITH RICE
9.	GAZPACHO	I.	COLD VEGETABLE SOUP
10.	SPOTTED DICK	J.	SWEET SUET PASTRY
11.	SAUER BRATEN	K.	SOUR ROASTED BEEF
12.	WIENER SCHNITZEL	L.	BREADED VEAL CUTLET
13.	BASHED NEEPS	M.	MASHED TURNIPS
14.	LE JAMBON	N.	HAM
15.	HUEVOS RANCHEROS	O.	RANCH STYLE EGGS
16.	OSSO BUCCO*	P.	STEWED VEAL SHANK
17.	PAIN AU CITRON	Q.	LEMON BREAD
18.	PASTA FAZOLLE**	R.	MACARONI AND BEAN SOUP
19.	PROSCIUTTO	S.	SPICY ITALIAN HAM
20.	OKTAPODI TOURSI	T.	PICKELED OCTOPUS
21.	HASENPFEFFER	U.	BRAISED RABBIT
22.	LE POISSON	V.	FISH
23.	FASTNACHTS	W.	DONUTS
24.	PETTO DE POLLO	X.	BREAST OF CHICKEN
25.	BUBBLE & SQUEEK	Y.	CABBAGE & MEAT MIX
26.	SOPA DE ALBONDIGUITAS	Z.	MEATBALL SOUP

* LIT. CLAY POT   ** ALSO FAGIOLI

BEERS OF THE WORLD

1.	AUSTRALIA	A.	FOSTER'S
2.	AUSTRIA	B.	EGGER LEICHT
3.	BAHAMAS	C.	KALIK
4.	BELGIUM	D.	STELLA ARTIOS
5.	CANADA	E.	LABATT'S
6.	CZECH REPUBLIC	F.	OSMA SURETLE
7.	DENMARK	G.	CARLSBERG
8.	ENGLAND	H.	WHITBREAD TROPHY
9.	GERMANY	I.	DINKEL ACKER
10.	HOLLAND	J.	HEINEKEN
11.	IRELAND	K.	GUINNESS STOUT
12.	ISRAEL	L.	MACCABEE
13.	ITALY	M.	LA ROSSA BIRRA
14.	JAMAICA	N.	RED STRIPE
15.	JAPAN	O.	SAPPORO
16.	MEXICO	P.	TECATE
17.	PERU	Q.	CUSQUENA
18.	PHILIPPINES	R.	SAN MIGUEL
19.	POLAND	S.	ZYWIEC
20.	SCOTLAND	T.	TENNENT'S
21.	SINGAPORE	U.	RAFFLE'S EXPORT
22.	THAILAND	V.	BLACK TIGER
23.	VIETNAM	W.	HUE BEER
24.	VIRGIN ISLANDS	X.	BLACK BEARD
25.	WALES	Y.	SNECK LIFFER
26.	WEST INDIES	Z.	CARIB LAGER

COCKTAILS ANYONE?

1.	SCREWDRIVER	A.	VODKA, ORANGE JUICE
2.	MARTINI	B.	GIN AND DRY VERMOUTH
3.	OLD FASHIONED	C.	BITTERS, MUDDLED FRUIT, SUGAR, RYE
4.	BLOODY MARY	D.	VODKA, TOMATO JUICE, SPICES
5.	STINGER	E.	BRANDY, CREME DE MENTHE
6.	MANHATTAN	F.	RYE AND SWEET VERMOUTH
7.	GIMLET	G.	GIN, SUGAR, LIME JUICE
8.	SOMBRERO	H.	KAHULA, CREAM
9.	MUDSLIDE	I.	VODKA, KAHULA, BAILEY'S
10.	ROB ROY	J.	SCOTCH, SWEET VERMOUTH
11.	DAIQUIRI	K.	RUM, SUGAR, SOUR MIX
12.	MINT JULEP	L.	BOURBON, MINT, WATER, SUGAR
13.	SALTY DOG	M.	VODKA, GRAPEFRUIT JUICE, SALT
14.	JACK ROSE	N.	APPLE JACK, SOUR MIX, GRENADINE
15.	TOM COLLINS	O.	GIN, SOUR MIX, CLUB SODA
16.	CUBA LIBRE	P.	RUM, COKE, LIME,
17.	GODFATHER	Q.	SCOTCH, AMARETTO
18.	MARGARITA	R.	TEQUILA, TRIPLE SEC, LIME JUICE
19.	FUZZY NAVAL	S.	PEACH SCHNAPPS, ORANGE JUICE
20.	MIMOSA	T.	CHAMPAGNE, ORANGE JUICE
21.	RUSTY NAIL	U.	SCOTCH, DRAMBUIE
22.	BLACK RUSSIAN	V.	VODKA, KAHLUA
23.	TOASTED ALMOND	W.	KAHULA, AMARETTO, CREAM
24.	BACARDI COCKTAIL	X.	RUM, SOUR MIX, GERNADINE
25.	B-52'S	Y.	GRAND MARINER, KAHULA, BAILEYS
26.	WOO WOO	Z.	VODKA, PEACH SCHNAPPS, CRANBERRY

"B" ON THE MAP

1.	BADEN-BADEN	A.	GERMANY
2.	BAHIA DE CUCHINOS	B.	CUBA
3.	BAGHDAD	C.	IRAQ
4.	BANFF	D.	CANADA
5.	BARCELONA	E.	SPAIN
6.	BARRANQUILLA	F.	COLUMBIA
7.	BATH	G.	ENGLAND
8.	BATON ROUGE	H.	USA
9.	BEIJING	I.	CHINA
10.	BEIRUT	J.	LEBANON
11.	BELFAST	K.	N. IRELAND
12.	BELGRADE	L.	YUGOSLAVIA
13.	BERGEN	M.	NORWAY
14.	BERN	N.	SWITZERLAND
15.	BIALYSTOK	O.	POLAND
16.	BIEN HOA	P.	VIETNAM
17.	BOMBAY	Q.	INDIA.
18.	BOLOGNA	R.	ITALY
19.	BORDEAUX	S.	FRANCE
20.	BRASILIA	T.	BRAZIL
21.	BRATISLAVA	U.	SLOVAKIA
22.	BRAZZAVILLE	V.	REPUBLIC OF THE CONGO
23.	BRISBANE	W.	AUSTRALIA
24.	BRUSSELLS	X.	BELGIUM
25.	BUCHAREST	Y.	ROMANIA
26.	BUDAPEST	Z.	HUNGARY

"M" ON THE MAP

1.	MADRAS	A.	INDIA
2.	MADRID	B.	SPAIN
3.	MALMO	C.	SWEDEN
4.	MANAGUA	D.	NICARAGUA
5.	MANCHESTER	E.	ENGLAND
6.	MANDALAY	F.	BURMA (MYANMAR)
7.	MANILA	G.	PHILIPPINES
8.	MARACAIBO	H.	VENEZUELA
9.	MARRAKECH	I.	MOROCCO
10.	MAZATLAN	J.	MEXICO
11.	MECCA	K.	SAUDI ARABIA
12.	MEDELLIN	L.	COLUMBIA
13.	MEDICINE HAT	M.	CANADA
14.	MELBOURNE	N.	AUSTRALIA
15.	MESSINA	O.	ITALY
16.	MINSK	P.	BELARUS
17.	MITO	Q.	JAPAN
18.	MOGADISHU	R.	SOMALIA
19.	MOMBASA	S.	KENYA
20.	MONROVIA	T.	LIBERIA
21.	MONTEVIDEO	U.	URUGUAY
22.	MONTE CARLO	V.	MONACO
23.	MONTPELIER	W.	USA
24.	MUNICH	X.	GERMANY
25.	MURMANSK	Y.	RUSSIA
26.	MUSCAT	Z.	OMAN

"S" ON THE MAP

1.	SAARBRUCKEN	A.	GERMANY
2.	SAIGON	B.	VIETNAM
3.	SAINT CROIX	C.	U. S. VIRGIN ISLANDS
4.	SALERNO	D.	ITALY
5.	SALISBURY	E.	RHODESIA
6.	SALONIKA	F.	GREECE
7.	SALZBURG	G.	AUSTRIA
8.	SAN JUAN	H.	PUERTO RICO
9.	SAN LUIS OBISPO	I.	USA
10.	SANTIAGO	J.	CHILE
11.	SAO PAULO	K.	BRAZIL
12.	SAPPORO	L.	JAPAN
13.	SARAJEVO	M.	BOSNIA
14.	SASKATOON	N.	CANADA
15.	SEOUL	O.	SOUTH KOREA
16.	SEVASTOPOL	P.	UKRAINE
17.	SEVILLE	Q.	SPAIN
18.	SHANGHAI	R.	CHINA
19.	SHETLAND ISLANDS	S.	SCOTLAND
20.	SOFIA	T.	BULGARIA
21.	SPITSBERGEN	U.	NORWAY
22.	STAFFORDSHIRE	V.	ENGLAND
23.	STOCKHOLM	W.	SWEDEN
24.	SUEZ	X.	EGYPT
25.	SUVA	Y.	FIJI
26.	SWANSEA	Z.	WALES

RIVERS & CITIES

1.	DELAWARE	A.	PHILADELPHIA, PA
2.	MISSISSIPPI	B.	MINNEAPOLIS, MN
3.	WHITE	C.	INDIANAPOLIS, IN
4.	OHIO	D.	LOUISVILLE, KY
5.	PENOBSCOT	E.	BANGOR, ME
6.	POTOMAC	F.	WASHINGTON, DC
7.	CHARLES	G.	BOSTON, MA
8.	MERRIMACK	H.	MANCHESTER, NH
9.	ARKANSAS	I.	TULSA, OK
10.	COLUMBIA	J.	PORTLAND, OR
11.	NILE	K.	CAIRO, EGYPT
12.	SEINE	L.	PARIS, FRANCE
13.	SCHUYLKILL	M.	READING, PA
14.	CUMBERLAND	N.	NASHVILLE, TN
15.	SOUTH CANADIAN	O.	OKLAHOMA CITY
16.	DANUBE	P.	VIENNA, AUSTRIA
17.	MONONGAHELA	Q.	DUQUESNE, PA
18.	RIO GRANDE	R.	EL PASO, TX
19.	LEHIGH	S.	ALLENTOWN, PA
20.	JAMES	T.	RICHMOND, VA
21.	THAMES	U.	LONDON, ENGLAND
22.	NIAGARA	V.	BUFFALO, NY
23.	SUSQUEHANNA	W.	HARRISBURG, PA
24.	NORTH PLATTE	X.	CASPER, WY
25.	TIBER	Y.	ROME, ITALY
26.	COLORADO	Z.	LAKE HAVASU CITY, AZ

WHERE ARE YOU FROM

1.	THE BIG APPLE	A.	NEW YORK, NY
2.	MILE HIGH CITY	B.	DENVER, CO
3.	WORLDS MOST FAMOUS BEACH	C.	DAYTONA BEACH,
4.	CITY OF FIVE SEASONS	D.	CEDAR RAPIDS, IA
5.	CITY OF LAKES	E.	MINNEAPOLIS, MN
6.	GATEWAY TO THE WEST	F.	ST. LOUIS, MO
7.	THE MOTOR CITY	G.	DETROIT, MI
8.	THE MUSIC CITY	H.	NASHVILLE, TN
9.	CITY OF BROTHERLY LOVE	I.	PHILA, PA
10.	THE BIG PEACH	J.	ATLANTA, GA
11.	CHARM CITY	K.	BALTIMORE, MD
12.	SOUL OF THE SOUTHWEST	L.	TAOS, NM
13.	SHOW CAPITOL OF THE WORLD	M.	LAS VEGAS, NV
14.	THE WINDY CITY	N.	CHICAGO, IL
15.	THE QUEEN CITY	O.	CINCINNATI, OH
16.	DERBYTOWN	P.	LOUISVILLE, KY
17.	THE EMERALD CITY	Q.	SEATTLE, WA
18.	THE CRESENT CITY	R.	NEW ORLEANS, LA
19.	THE CITY BY THE BAY	S.	SAN FRANCISCO, CA
20.	THE CIRCLE CITY	T.	INDIANAPOLIS, IN
21.	THE CITY OF ANGELS	U.	LOS ANGELES, CA
22.	THE ANCIENT CITY	V.	ST AUGUSTINE, FL
23.	BEANTOWN	W.	BOSTON, MA
24.	VALLEY OF THE SUN	X.	PHOENIX, AZ
25.	THE CITY OF TREES	Y.	BOISE, ID
26.	THE BIGGEST LITTLE CITY IN THE WORLD	Z.	RENO, NV

U.S. STATE NICKNAMES

1.	ALASKA	A.	THE LAST FRONTIER
2.	ARKANSAS	B.	THE NATURAL STATE
3.	CALIFORNIA	C.	THE GOLDEN STATE
4.	COLORADO	D.	THE CENTENIAL STATE
5.	CONNECTICUT	E.	THE CONSTITUTION STATE
6.	DELAWARE	F.	THE DIAMOND STATE
7.	GEORGIA	G.	THE PEACH STATE
8.	IDAHO	H.	THE GEM STATE
9.	IOWA	I.	THE HAWKEYE STATE
10.	KANSAS	J.	THE SUNFLOWER STATE
11.	LOUISIANA	K.	THE PELICAN STATE
12.	MAINE	L.	THE PINE TREE STATE
13.	MARYLAND	M.	THE OLD LINE STATE
14.	MASSACHUSETTS	N.	THE BAY STATE
15.	MINNESOTA	O.	THE NORTH STAR STATE
16.	MISSISSIPPI	P.	THE MAGNOLIA STATE
17.	MONTANA	Q.	THE TREASURE STATE
18.	NEVADA	R.	THE SILVER STATE
19.	NEW HAMPSHIRE	S.	THE GRANITE STATE
20.	NEW JERSEY	T.	THE GARDEN STATE
21.	NEW MEXICO	U.	THE LAND OF ENCHANTMENT
22.	OREGON	V.	THE BEAVER STATE
23.	PENNA.	W.	THE KEYSTONE STATE
24.	UTAH	X.	THE BEEHIVE STATE
25.	VIRGINIA	Y.	THE OLD DOMINION STATE
26.	WYOMING	Z.	THE EQUALITY STATE (ALSO COWBOY)

STATE CAPITOLS

1.	ALABAMA	A.	MONGTOMERY
2.	ARKANSAS	B.	LITTLE ROCK
3.	IDAHO	C.	BOISE
4.	ILLINOIS	D.	SPRINGFIELD
5.	IOWA	E.	DES MOINES
6.	KANSAS	F.	TOPEKA
7.	KENTUCKY	G.	FRANKFORT
8.	LOUISIANA	H.	BATON ROUGE
9.	MAINE	I.	AUGUSTA
10.	MARYLAND	J.	ANNAPOLIS
11.	MICHIGAN	K.	LANSING
12.	MINNESOTA	L.	ST. PAUL
13.	MISSISSIPPI	M.	JACKSON
14.	MISSOURI	N.	JEFFERSON CITY
15.	MONTANA	O.	HELENA
16.	NEBRASKA	P.	LINCOLN
17.	NEVADA	Q.	CARSON CITY
18.	NEW HAMPSHIRE	R.	CONCORD
19.	NORTH DAKOTA	S.	BISMARCK
20.	OREGON	T.	SALEM
21.	SOUTH CAROLINA	U.	COLUMBIA
22.	SOUTH DAKOTA	V.	PIERRE
23.	VERMONT	W.	MONTPELIER
24.	WASHINGTON	X.	OLYMPIA
25.	WEST VIRGINIA	Y.	CHARLESTON
26.	WISCONSIN	Z.	MADISON

NATIONAL PARKS BY STATE

1.	SARATOGA NAT'L HISTORICAL PARK	A.	NEW YORK
2.	EVERGLADES NAT'L PARK	B.	FLORIDA
3.	ACADIA NATIONAL PARK	C.	MAINE
4.	VICKSBURG NATIONAL PARK	D.	MISSISSIPPI
5.	ZION NATIONAL PARK	E.	UTAH
6.	HARPER'S FERRY NAT'L HISTORY PARK	F.	WEST VIRGINIA
7.	YELLOWSTONE NATIONAL PARK	G.	WYOMING
8.	BADLANDS NAT'L PARK	H.	SOUTH DAKOTA
9.	PETRIFIED FOREST NAT'L PARK	I.	ARIZONA
10.	ANDERSONVILLE NAT'L HIST SITE	J.	GEORGIA
11.	JEAN LAFITE NAT'L PARK	K.	LOUISIANA
12.	VALLEY FORGE NAT'L HIST PARK	L.	PENNSYLVANIA
13.	NEZ PERCE NAT'L HIST PARK	M.	IDAHO
14.	MOUNT RAINIER NAT'L PARK	N.	WASHINGTON
15.	FORT SUMTER NAT'L MONUMENT	O.	SOUTH CAROLINA
16.	ANTIETAM NAT'L CEMETERY	P.	MARYLAND
17.	CRATER LAKE NAT'L PARK	Q.	OREGON
18.	VOYAGEURS NAT'L PARK	R.	MINNESOTA
19.	CARLSBAD CAVERNS NAT'L PARK	S.	NEW MEXICO
20.	BIG BEND NAT'L PARK	T.	TEXAS
21.	YOSEMITE NAT'L PARK	U.	CALIFORNIA
22.	SHENANDOAH NAT'L PARK	V.	VIRGINIA
23.	GREAT BASIN NAT'L PARK	W.	NEVADA
24.	HOT SPRINGS NAT'L PARK	X.	ARKANSAS
25.	DENALI NAT'L PARK	Y.	ALASKA
26.	MAMOTH CAVE NATIONAL PARK	Z.	KENTUCKY

TOURIST TRAPS

1.	THE LIBERTY BELL		A.	PHILA, PA
2.	GRANT'S TOMB		B.	NEW YORK, NY
3.	THE SPACE NEEDLE		C.	SEATTLE, WA
4.	THE GATEWAY ARCH		D.	ST. LOUIS, MO
5.	"GRACE LAND"		E.	MEMPHIS, TN
6.	THE PRESIDIO		F.	SAN FRANCISCO, CA
7.	SEARS TOWER		G.	CHICAGO, IL
8.	FANEUIL HALL		H.	BOSTON, MA
9.	(HMS) QUEEN MARY		I.	LONG BEACH, CA
10.	PIKES PEAK		J.	COLORADO SPRINGS, CO
11.	THE ALAMO		K.	SAN ANTONIO, TX
12.	HOOVER DAM		L.	LAS VEGAS, NV
13.	FORT SUMTER		M.	CHARLESTON, SC
14.	MT. RUSHMORE		N.	RAPID CITY, SC
15.	E. A. POES GRAVE		O.	BALTIMORE, MD
16.	MAMMOTH CAVE		P.	BOWLING GREEN, KY
17.	THE ROSE BOWL		Q.	PASADENA, CA
18.	THE LONDON BRIDGE		R.	LAKE HAVASU CITY, AZ
19.	"THE BRICKYARD"		S.	INDIANAPOLIS
20.	USS ARIZONA MEMORIAL		T.	HONOLULU, HI
21.	"FRENCH QUARTER"		U.	NEW ORLEANS
22.	CHURCHILL DOWNS		V.	LOUISVILLE, KY
23.	THE TOMB OF THE UNKNOWN SOLIDER		W.	ARLINGTON, VA
24.	STONE MOUNTAIN		X.	ATLANTA, GA
25.	THE SMITHSONIAN INST.		Y.	WASHINGTON DC
26.	THE EXPERIMENTAL PROTOTYPE COMMUNITY OF TOMORROW		Z.	ORLANDO, FL

I FLEW TO CHICAGO HOW DID MY BAGS GET TO PARIS?

1.	LAX	A.	LOS ANGELES INTL
2.	LHR	B.	LONDON'S HEATHROW
3.	SLC	C.	SALT LAKE CITY, UT
4.	SNN	D.	SHANNON, IRELAND
5.	ORY	E.	PARIS, FRANCE
6.	ABQ	F.	ALBUQUERQUE, NM
7.	BWI	G.	BALTIMORE, MD
8.	SJU	H.	SAN JUAN, PUERTO RICO
9.	MCO	I.	ORLANDO, FL
10.	ORD	J.	CHICAGO, IL (O'HARE)
11.	DFW	K.	DALLAS, TX
12.	EWR	L.	NEWARK, NJ
13.	MKC	M.	KANSAS CITY, MO
14.	DCA	N.	WASHINGTON DC (NATIONAL)
15.	NRT	O.	TOYKO, JAPAN
16.	IAH	P.	HOUSTON, TX
17.	PHX	Q.	PHOENIX, AZ
18.	HNL	R.	HONOLULU, HI
19.	ABE	S.	ALLENTOWN, PA
20.	LAS	T.	LAS VEGAS, NV
21.	FCO	U.	ROME, ITALY
22.	SFO	V.	SAN FRANCISCO, CA
23.	MSP	W.	MINNEAPOLIS, MN
24.	LGA	X.	NEW YORK, NY (LAGUARDIA)
25.	HKG	Y.	HONG KONG
26.	SJC	Z.	SAN JOSE, CA

MATCH THE CAPITOL CITY TO

IT'S COUNTRY

1.	IRELAND	A.	DUBLIN
2.	EGYPT	B.	CAIRO
3.	URUGUAY	C.	MONTEVIDEO
4.	CANADA	D.	OTTAWA
5.	POLAND	E.	WARSAW
6.	SPAIN	F.	MADRID
7.	PORTUGAL	G.	LISBON
8.	FINLAND	H.	HELSINKI
9.	SWEDEN	I.	STOCKHOLM
10.	WALES	J.	CARDIFF
11.	AUSTRALIA	K.	CANBERRA
12.	PHILIPPINES	L.	MANILA
13.	COLUMBIA	M.	BOGOTA
14.	IRAN	N.	TEHRAN
15.	PERU	O.	LIMA
16.	CHILE	P.	SANTIAGO
17.	LIBERIA	Q.	MONROVIA
18.	IRAQ	R.	BAGHDAD
19.	LIBYA	S.	TRIPOLI
20.	MOROCCO	T.	RABAT
21.	THAILAND	U.	BANGKOK
22.	KENYA	V.	NAIROBI
23.	SOUTH KOREA	W.	SEOUL
24.	INDIA	X.	NEW DELHI
25.	AUSTRIA	Y.	VIENNA
26.	BELGIUM	Z.	BRUSSELS

WORLD LEADERS

THEN AND NOW

1.	ARGENTINA	A.	JUAN PERON
2.	CANADA	B.	PIERRE ELLIOT TRUDEAU
3.	CHINA	C.	MAO TSE TUNG
4.	CUBA	D.	FIDEL CASTRO
5.	EGYPT	E.	ANWAR SADAT
6.	ENGLAND	F.	WINSTON CHURCHILL
7.	FRANCE	G.	CHARLES DE GAULLE
8.	INDIA	H.	INDIRA GANDHI
9.	IRAN	I.	AYATOLLAH KHOMEINI
10.	IRAQ	J.	SADDAM HUSSEIN
11.	IRELAND	K.	EAMON DE VALERA
12.	ISRAEL	L.	GOLDA MEIR
13.	ITALY	M.	BENITO MUSSOLINI
14.	JAPAN	N.	EMPEROR HIROHITO
15.	NORTH KOREA	O.	KIM IL SUNG
16.	LIYBA	P.	MUAMMAR AL QADDAFI
17.	MEXICO	Q.	VICENTE FOX
18.	PANAMA	R.	MANUEL NORIEGA
19.	PERU	S.	ALBERTO FUJIMORI
20.	PHILIPPINES	T.	CORAZON AQUINO
21.	POLAND	U.	LECH WALESA
22.	RUSSIA	V.	BORIS YELTSIN
23.	SPAIN	W.	FRANCISCO FRANCO
24.	SOUTH AFRICA	X.	NELSON MANDELA
25.	UGANDA	Y.	IDI AMIN
26.	UNITED STATES	Z.	DWIGHT D EISENHOWER

EUROPEAN TRAVELS

1.	OUI, MERCI BEACOUP	A.	YES, THANK YOU VERY MUCH
2.	PARLEZ-VOUS ANGLAIS.	B.	DO YOU SPEAK ENGLISH?
3.	SPRECHEN SIE DEUTSCH	C.	DO YOU SPEAK GERMAN?
4.	AUF WIEDERSEHEN	D.	GOOD BYE
5.	CEDE MIL FALTE	E.	100,000 WELCOMES
6.	NON CAPISCO	F.	I DON'T UNDERSTAND
7.	BUON GIORNO	G.	GOOD MORNING
8.	GOEDENACHT.	H.	GOOD NIGHT
9.	WAAR IS.	I.	WHERE IS
10.	VELKOMMEN	J.	WELCOME
11.	TAKK	K.	THANK YOU
12.	QUARTO DE BANHO	L.	BATHROOM
13.	AUTOCARRO	M.	BUS
14.	PRAVDA	N.	TRUTH
15.	UNA CERVEZA, POR FAVOR	O.	ONE BEER PLEASE
16.	DONDE ESTA LOS SERVICIOS.	P.	WHERE IS THE MENS ROOM?
17.	SKAL	Q.	TO YOUR HEALTH
18.	KAN JAG BETALA MED KREDITKORT	R.	DO YOU TAKE CREDIT CARDS
19.	BROLLY	S.	UMBRELLA
20.	BOOT	T.	CAR TRUNK

FOREIGN MONEY

(PRIOR TO EUROS)

1.	ARGENTINA		A.	PESOS
2.	AUSTRIA		B.	SCHILLINGS
3.	BELGIUM		C.	FRANCS
4.	CHINA		D.	YUAN
5.	DENMARK		E.	KRONER
6.	GERMANY		F.	MARKS
7.	GREECE		G.	DRACHMA
8.	HUNGARY		H.	FORINT
9.	INDONESIA		I.	RUPIAHS
10.	ISREAL		J.	SHEKELS
11.	ITALY		K.	LIRA
12.	JAPAN		L.	YEN
13.	JORDAN		M.	DINAR
14.	KOREA		N.	WON
15.	MAYLAYSIA		O.	RINGGITS
16.	NETHERLANDS		P.	GUILDERS
17.	POLAND		Q.	ZLOTY
18.	PORTUGAL		R.	ESCUDOS
19.	RUMANIA		S.	LEI
20.	SAUDI ARABIA		T.	RIYAL
21.	SOUTH AFRICA		U.	RAND
22.	SPAIN		V.	PESETAS
23.	U.K.		W.	POUNDS
24.	RUSSIA		X.	RUBLES
25.	INDIA		Y.	RUPEES
26.	VENEZULA		Z.	BOLIVAR

FOREIGN TRAVELS

1.	ABBEY THEATER	A.	DUBLIN, IRELAND
2.	DURTY NELLY'S	B.	SHANNON, IRELAND
3.	BIG BEN	C.	LONDON, ENG
4.	STONEHENGE	D.	SALISBURY PLAIN, ENG
5.	ARC DE TRIUMPHE	E.	PARIS, FRANCE
6.	HALL OF MIRRORS	F.	VERSAILLES, FRANCE
7.	SISTINE CHAPEL	G.	VATICAN CITY
8.	TREVI FOUNTAIN	H.	ROME, ITALY
9.	DACHAU	I.	MUNICH, GERMANY
10.	THE REICHESTAG	J.	BERLIN, GERMANY
11.	THE ALHAMBRA	K.	GRANADA, SPAIN
12.	THE PRADO	L.	MADRID, SPAIN
13.	THE ACROPOLIS	M.	ATHENS, GREECE
14.	THE HERMITAGE	N.	SAINT PETERSBURG, RUSSIA
15.	BONDY BEACH	O.	SYDNEY, AUSTRALIA
16.	AYERS ROCK	P.	ALICE SPRINGS, AUSTRALIA
17.	TIGER BALM GARDENS	Q.	SINGAPORE
18.	THE STAR FERRY	R.	HONG KONG
19.	THE GINZA	S.	TOKYO, JAPAN
20.	THE TAJ MAHAL	T.	AGRA, INDIA
21.	MOUNT KILIMANJARO	U.	TANZANIA, AFRICA
22.	TIANAMEN SQUARE	V.	BEIJING, CHINA
23.	THE WAILING WALL	W.	JERUSALEM
24.	CN TOWER	X.	TOTONTO, CANADA
25.	PLAINS OF ABRAHAM	Y.	QUEBEC CITY, PQ CANADA
26.	IPANEMA BEACH	Z.	RIO DE JANERIO, BRAZIL

FOREIGN PHRASES

1.	ANNUS MIRABLIS	A.	A GREAT YEAR
2.	A PRIORI	B.	BASED ON THEORY
3.	AU COURANT	C.	UP TO DATE
4.	BONA FIDE	D.	GENIUNE
5.	BON MOT	E.	A WITTY REMARK
6.	BON VIVANT	F.	ONE WHO ENJOYS LIFE
7.	CARPE DIEM	G.	SEIZE THE DAY
8.	CAVEAT EMPTOR	H.	LET THE BUYER BEWARE
9.	COMME CI COMME CA	I.	SO SO
10.	COMME IL FAUT	J.	AS IT SHOULD BE
11.	COUPE DE GRACE	K.	FINISHING BLOW
12.	LA DOLCE VITA	L.	THE SWEET LIFE
13.	ENFANT TERRIBLE	M.	A BRAT
14.	ENTRE NOUS	N.	BETWEEN US
15.	FAIT ACCOMPLI	O.	ALREADY DONE
16.	FAUX PAS	P.	SOCIAL BLUNDER
17.	FLAGRANTE DELICTO	Q.	IN THE ACT
18.	HOI POLLOI	R.	THE COMMON PEOPLE
19.	IN LOCO PARENTIS	S.	IN PLACE OF PARENTS
20.	IN VINO VERITAS	T.	IN WINE THERE IS TRUTH
21.	JE NE SAIS QUOI	U.	AN ELUSIVE QUALITY (lit. I do not know what)
22.	MANO A MANO	V.	FACE TO FACE
23.	MEA CULPA	W.	I AM AT FAULT
24.	PERSONA NON GRATA	X.	UNWELCOME PERSON
25.	PRO BONO	Y.	AT NO CHARGE
26.	VOX POPULI	Z.	VOICE OF THE PEOPLE

MORE FOREIGN WORDS & PHRASES

1.	AD NAUSEAM	A.	TO A SICKENING DEGREE
2.	AFICIONADO	B.	A DEVOTED FOLLOWER
3.	BEAU GESTE	C.	A NOBLE GESTURE
4.	BETE NOIR	D.	DISLIKED PERSON OR THING
5.	CARTE BLANCHE	E.	UNRESTRICTED POWER OR USE
6.	CRI DE COEUR	F.	APPEAL FROM THE HEART
7.	DE RIGUEUR	G.	REQUIRED BY ETIQUETTE
8.	EX CATHEDRA	H.	FROM THE CHAIR
9.	EX POST FACTO	I.	DONE BUT RETROACTIVE
10.	J' ACCUSE	J.	I MAKE AN ACCUSATION
11.	IN VITRO	K.	IN GLASS
12.	IPSO FACTO	L.	BY THE FACT
13.	MODUS OPERANDI	M.	A WAY OF DOING SOMETHING
14.	NOBLESSE OBLIGE	N.	DUTY TO HELP LESS WELL OFF
15.	NOM DE PLUME	O.	A PEN NAME
16.	QUID PRO QUO	P.	AN EQUAL EXCHANGE
17.	SAN SOUCI	Q.	WITHOUT WORRY
18.	SEMPER FIDELIS	R.	ALWAYS FAITHFUL
19.	SIC SEMPER TYRANNIS	S.	THUS ALWAYS TO TYRANTS
20.	SAVOIR-FAIRE	T.	ABILITY TO DO IT RIGHT
21.	TOUTE DE SUITE	U.	RIGHT NOW
22.	TOUTE LE MONDE	V.	EVERYONE IN THE WORLD
23.	SINE QUA NON	W.	CAN'T DO WITHOUT
24.	VICI	X.	I CONQUERED
25.	VIDI	Y.	I SAW
26.	VINI	Z.	I CAME

ALL THINGS MILITARY

1.	ACE	A.	PILOT WITH 5 KILLS
2.	ACK-ACK	B.	ANTI-AIRCRAFT FIRE
3.	BULKHEAD	C.	WALL ON A SHIP
4.	F-4 PHANTOM	D.	FIGHTER JET
5.	ENOLA GAY	E.	DROPPED FIRST A BOMB
6.	FATIGUES	F.	WORK UNIFORM
7.	FLANK	G.	ENCIRCLING MOTION
8.	FLAT TOP	H.	AIRCRAFT CARRIER
9.	FUBAR	I.	SNAFU
10.	CINCPAC	J.	NAVY BOSS PACIFIC FLEET
11.	DEUCE + A HALF	K.	ARMY TRUCK
12.	GEEDUNK	L.	JUNK FOOD OR STORE
13.	GITMO	M.	GUANTANAMO BAY CUBA
14.	H-1 HUEY	N.	LARGE HELICOPTER
15.	LIBERTY	O.	SAILORS DAY OFF ASHORE
16.	JN 25	P.	JAPANESE NAVAL CODE
17.	M-1	Q.	BASIC WW2 ARMY RIFLE
18.	MP'S	R.	THE ARMY'S COPS
19.	MAE WEST	S.	A LIFE JACKET
20.	PX	T.	ARMY OR AIR FORCE BASE STORE
21.	SCUTTLEBUTT	U.	DRINKING FOUNTAIN/NAVY
22.	SHELLBACK	V.	SAILOR WHO HAS CROSSED THE EQUATOR
23.	OVERLORD	W.	D-DAY PLAN CODE NAME
24.	SR7I BLACKBIRD	X.	FASTEST JET EVER
25.	SHERMAN	Y.	AMERICAN WW2 TANK
26.	ZERO	Z.	JAPANESE WW2 PLANE

INVENTORS & DISCOVERERS

1.	IGOR SIKORSKI	A.	HELICOPTER
2.	SAMUEL MORSE	B.	TELEGRAPH CODE
3.	PHILO T. FARNSWORTH	C.	TV TUBE
4.	ELIAS HOWE	D.	SEWING MACHINE
5.	JAMES WATT	E.	STEAM ENGINE
6.	JETHRO TULL	F.	SEED PLANTER
7.	BEN FRANKLIN	G.	BIFOCAL LENSES
8.	THOMAS EDISON	H.	PHONOGRAPH
9.	GEORGE WESTINGHOUSE	I.	AIRBRAKE
10.	ELI WHITNEY	J.	COTTON GIN
11.	ALEXANDER FLEMING	K.	PENICILLIN
12.	HENRY FORD	L.	ASESSEMBLY LINE
13.	HENRY BESSEMER	M.	BLAST FURNACE
14.	A.G. BELL	N.	TELEPHONE
15.	JAQUES COUSTEAU	O.	AQUALUNG
16.	EDWIN LAND	P.	INSTANT PICTURES
17.	G. MARCONI	Q.	RADIO
18.	JOHN DEERE	R.	CAST STEEL PLOW
19.	ROBERT GODDARD	S.	ROCKET CONTROLS
20.	WILLIAM LEAR	T.	CAR RADIO & 8 TRACK
21.	E.G. OTIS	U.	ELEVATOR BRAKE
22.	LOUIS PASTEUR	V.	STABLE BEER
23.	CHARLES GOODYEAR	W.	VULCANIZED RUBBER
24.	ENRICO FERMI	X.	NEUTRON REACTOR
25.	SEYMOUR CRAY	Y.	SUPER COMPUTER
26.	FELIX WANKEL	Z.	ROTARY ENGINE

IT HAPPENED WHEN?

1.	MAN WALKS ON MOON	A.	1969
2.	FALL OF BERLIN WALL	B.	1989
3.	START OF WW II	C.	1939
4.	DEBUT OF THE EDSEL	D.	1957
5.	DEATH OF JFK	E.	1963
6.	FOUR MINUTE MILE BROKEN	F.	1954
7.	DESERT STORM HITS IRAQ	G.	1991
8.	BEATLES ON ED SULLIVAN	H.	1964
9.	DEATH OF M L KING JR.	I.	1968
10.	REPEAL OF PROHIBITION	J.	1933
11.	FIRST AIRPLANE FLIGHT	K.	1903
12.	PEARL HARBOR ATTACKED	L.	1941
13.	CLINTON IMPEACHED	M.	1998
14.	FIRST HEART TRANSPLANT	N.	1967
15.	STOCK MARKET CRASHES	O.	1929
16.	DEATH OF ELVIS PRESLEY	P.	1977
17.	HAWAII GAINS STATEHOOD	Q.	1959
18.	DEATH OF HRH DIANA	R.	1997
19.	MODEL T INTRODUCED	S.	1908
20.	ELIZABETH II CROWNED	T.	1953
21.	TRUMAN DEFEATS DEWEY	U.	1948
22.	INVASION OF NORMANDY	V.	1944
23.	LANDING AT INCHON	W.	1950
24.	"A BOMBING OF HIROSHIMA	X.	1945

WHO SAID IT?

1. ASK NOT WHAT YOUR COUNTRY CAN DO FOR YOU
2. I SHALL RETURN
3. GIVE ME LIBERTY OR GIVE DEATH
4. I SHALL GO TO KOREA
5. WE HAVE NOTHING TO FEAR BUT FEAR ITSELF
6. I HAVE NOT YET BEGUN TO FIGHT
7. I AM NOT A CROOK
8. ONE SMALL STEP FOR MAN
9. I SHALL NOT SEEK AND I WILL NOT ACCEPT MY PARTYS NOMINATION
10. NUTS
11. READ MY LIPS, NO NEW TAXES
12. MEN SHALL STILL SAY, THIS WAS THEIR FINEST HOUR
13. IT AIN'T OVER TILL IT'S OVER
14. IF YOU CAN'T STAND THE HEAT GET OUT OF THE KITCHEN
15. THIS WAY TO THE EGRESS
16. MR. GORBACHOV, TEAR DOWN THIS WALL
17. GOV. OF THE PEOPLE BY THE PEOPLE FOR THE PEOPLE
18. EARLY TO BED, EARLY TO RISE.
19. TUNE IN, TURN ON, DROP OUT
20. SPEAK SOFTLY, AND CARRY A BIG STICK
21. I FEAR ALL WE HAVE DONE IS AWAKEN A SLEEPING GIANT
22. NOW I HAVE BECOME DEATH

A. JOHN F KENNEDY
B. DOUGLAS MC ARTHUR
C. PATRICK HENRY
D. D. D. EISENHOWER

E. FRANKLIN D. ROOSEVELDT
F. JOHN PAUL JONES
G. RICHARD NIXON
H. NEIL ARMSTRONG

I. LYNDON B. JOHNSON
J. W. A. MCAULIFFE
K. GEORGE H. W. BUSH

L. WINSTON CHURCHILL
M. YOGI BERRA

N. HARRY TRUMAN
O. P. T. BARNUM

P. RONALD REAGAN

Q. ABRAHAM LINCOLN
R. BEN FRANKLIN
S. TIMOTHY LEARY
T. TEDDY ROOSEVELDT
U. HIDEKI TOJO
V. ROBERT OPPENHEIMER

23. I DID NOT HAVE SEX
    WITH THAT WOMAN   W.   WILLIAM CLINTON
24. DR. LIVINGSTONE, I PRESUME   X.   H. M. STANLEY
25. I HAVE LUSTED AFTER
    WOMEN IN MY HEART.   Y.   JIMMY CARTER
26. ON THE WHOLE,
    I'D RATHER BE IN PHILADELPHIA   Z.   W.C. FIELDS

THE BOYS AND GIRLS IN THE BAND

1.	THE MIRACLES	A.	SMOKEY ROBINSON
2.	THE BEE GEES	B.	MAURICE GIBB
3.	THE FOUR SEASONS	C.	FRANKIE VALLI
4.	NIRVANA	D.	KURT COBAIN
5.	THE STONE PONYS	E.	LINDA RONSTADT
6.	THE BELMONTS	F.	DION DIMUCCI
7.	GUNS AND ROSES	G.	AXEL ROSE
8.	THE UNION GAP	H.	GARY PUCKETT
9.	MAMAS AND PAPAS	I.	CASS ELLIOT
10.	THE BEATLES	J.	RICHARD STARKEY
11.	THE DIXIE CHICKS	K.	EMILY ERWIN
12.	ROLLING STONES	L.	KEITH RICHARDS
13.	THE MONKEES	M.	PETER TORK
14.	ZZ TOP	N.	DUSTY HILL
15.	THE E STREET BAND	O.	STEVEN VAN ZANDT
16.	CREED	P.	SCOTT STAPP
17.	THE MARVELETTES	Q.	WANDA ROGERS
18.	THE TEMPTATIONS	R.	OTIS WILLIAMS
19.	BACK STREET BOYS	S.	A. J. MCLEAN
20.	THE 5TH DIMENSION	T.	MARILYN MCCOO
21.	THE SUPREMES	U.	MARY WILSON
22.	IN SYNC	V.	LANCE BASS
23.	NO DOUBT	W.	GWEN STEFFANI
24.	BEASTIE BOYS	X.	MIX MASTER MIKE
25.	THE BEACH BOYS	Y.	GLEN CAMPBELL
26.	CCR	Z.	JOHN FOGERTY

MUSIC VIDEOS

1.	THRILLER	A.	MICHAEL JACKSON
2.	MY HEART WILL GO ON	B.	CELINE DION
3.	ONE	C.	METALLICA
4.	1979	D.	SMASHING PUMPKINS
5.	STEPPIN OUT	E.	TONY BENNETT
6.	SMELLS LIKE TEEN SPIRIT	F.	NIRVANA
7.	ADDICTED TO LOVE	G.	ROBERT PALMER
8.	IRONIC	H.	A. MORISSETTE
9.	GIRLS JUST WANT TO HAVE FUN	I.	CINDY LAUPER
10.	WILD THANG	J.	TONE LOC
11.	LOVE SHACK	K.	B52'S
12.	FREEDOM	L.	GEORGE MICHAEL
13.	WANTED DEAD/ALIVE	M.	BON JOVI
14.	WHAT A GIRL WANTS	N.	C. AGULARIA
15.	1999	O.	PRINCE
16.	WHIP IT	P.	DEVO
17.	CANDLE IN THE WIND	Q.	ELTON JOHN
18.	GIMME ALL YOUR LOVIN	R.	ZZ TOP
19.	RHYTHM NATION	S.	JANET JACKSON
20.	JUST A GIGOLO	T.	DAVID LEE ROTH
21.	GIN AND JUICE	U.	SNOOP DOGG
22.	UPTOWN GIRL	V.	BILLY JOEL
23.	FAKE PLASTIC TREES	W.	RADIOHEAD
24.	RENEE	X.	LOST BOYZ
25.	LIKE A VIRGIN	Y.	MADONNA
26.	ARMS WIDE OPEN	Z.	CREED

CITIES IN SONGS

1.	I LEFT MY HEART IN	A.	SAN FRANCISCO
2.	I'VE GOT A GIRL IN	B.	KALAMAZOO
3.	THERE IS A HOUSE IN	C.	NEW ORLEANS
4.	THE LAST TIME I SAW	D.	PARIS
5.	OUT IN THE WEST TEXAS TOWN OF	E.	EL PASO
6.	ON THE STREETS OF	F.	PHILADELPHIA
7.	MY CHINA DOLL DOWN IN OLD	G.	HONG KONG
8.	IT'S UP TO YOU	H.	NEW YORK, NEW YORK
9.	THE KIDS IN	I.	BRISTOL
10.	I'M GOING TO	J.	KANSAS CITY
11.	MIDNITE TRAIN//DESTINATION	K.	BANGOR, MAINE
12.	DO YOU KNOW THE WAY TO	L.	SAN JOSE
13.	BY THE TIME I GET TO	M.	PHOENIX
14.	ON THE ATCHISON, TOPEKA AND	N.	SANTA FE
15.	MY KIND OF TOWN	O.	CHICAGO
16.	I SHOT A MAN IN	P.	RENO
17.	LAST NITE I WENT TO SLEEP IN	Q.	DETROIT CITY
18.	THERE'S 1352 GUITAR PICKERS	R.	NASHVILLE
19.	ON THE WAY TO	S.	CAPE MAY
20.	GOING BACK TO	T.	HOUSTON
21.	PARDON ME BOY, IS THAT THE	U.	CHATTANOOGA
22.	MEET ME IN	V.	ST. LOUIS
23.	ARRIVEDERCI	W.	ROMA
24.	HELP ME INFORMATION, GET ME	X.	MEMPHIS
25.	I'M AT WKRP IN	Y.	CINCINNATI
26.	VIVA	Z.	LAS VEGAS

WW2 ERA SONGS

1.	WHEN YOU WISH UPON A STAR	A.	WILL COME TO YOU
2.	CHATTANOOGA CHOO CHOO	B.	PARDON ME, BOY
3.	DEEP IN THE HEART OF TEXAS	C.	BIG AND BRIGHT
4.	DON'T SIT UNDER THE APPLE TREE	D.	TIL I COME MARCHIN HOMEE
5.	WHITE CLIFFS OF DOVER	E.	BLUEBIRDS OVER
6.	AS TIME GOES BY	F.	TWO LOVERS WOO
7.	PAPER DOLL	G.	FLIRTY FLIRTY EYES
8.	DON'T FENCE ME IN	H.	STARRY SKIES ABOVE
9.	I'LL BE SEEING YOU	I.	OLD FAMILIAR PLACES
10.	MAIRZY DOATS	J.	LAMBS EAT IVY
11.	SWINGING ON A STAR	K.	RATHER BE A MULE
12.	IT'S BEEN A LONG LONG TIME	L.	KISS ME TWICE
13.	RUM AND COCA-COLA	M.	YANKEE DOLLAR
14.	SENTIMENTAL JOURNEY	N.	GONNA TAKE A
15.	AC-CENT-TCHU-ATE THE POSTIVE	O.	MISTER IN BETWEEN
16.	WHITE CHRISTMAS	P.	CHILDREN LISTEN
17.	OVER THE RAINBOW	Q.	IN A LULLABY
18.	THANKS FOR THE MEMORY	R.	HOW LOVELY IT WAS
19.	BILL BAILEY	S.	FINE TOOTH COMB
20.	CATCH A FALLING STAR	T.	IN YOUR POCKET
21.	IN HEAVEN THERE IS NO	U.	WE DRINK IT HERE
22.	STARDUST	V.	HAUNTS MY REVERIE
23.	THOSE LAZY HAZY CRAZY DAYS	W.	SODA + PRETZELS + BEER
24.	YOUNG AT HEART	X.	TO ONE HUNDRED AND FIVE
25.	LILY MARLENE	Y.	UNDERN'TH THE LAMP LIGHT
26.	GOD BLESS AMERICA	Z.	WHITE WITH FOAM

MERRY CHRISTMAS JOYEUX NOEL

1.	SILENT NIGHT	A.	ROUND YON VIRGIN
2.	HARK THE HERALD ANGELS	B.	AND MERCY MILD
3.	O COME ALL YE FAITHFUL	C.	JOYFUL & TRIUMPHANT
4.	THE FIRST NOEL	D.	CERTAIN POOR SHEPHERDS
5.	GO TELL IT ON THE MOUNTAIN	E.	AND EVERYWHERE
6.	LITTLE DRUMMER BOY	F.	I HAVE NO GIFT TO BRING
7.	O LITTLE TOWN OF BETHLEHEM	G.	THE EVERLASTING LIGHT
8.	COME TO THE MANGER	H.	YOU'LL FORGET YOUR FLOCKS
9.	HANDEL'S MESSIAH	I.	HE SHALL REIGN FOREVER
10.	WHAT CHILD IS THIS	J.	WHERE OX & ASS/FEEDING
11.	GOD REST YOU MERRY, GENTLEMAN	K.	TO SAVE US ALL
12.	ANGELS WE HAVE HEARD	L.	IN EXCELSIS DEO
13.	AWAY IN A MANGER	M.	ASLEEP ON THE HAY
14.	IT CAME UPON A MIDNIGHT CLEAR	N.	HARPS OF GOLD
15.	RISE UP SHEPHERD	O.	HE LIES 'MID THE BEASTS
16.	ANGELS FROM THE REALMS OF GLORY	P.	SAINTS BEFORE THE ALTAR BENDING
17.	GOOD KING WENCESLAS	Q.	DEEP & CRISP & EVEN
18.	I SAW THREE SHIPS	R.	ON CHRISTMAS DAY IN THE MORNING
19.	JOY TO THE WORLD	S.	RECEIVE HER KING
20.	O HOLY NIGHT	T.	WEARY WORLD REJOICES
21.	DO YOU HEAR WHAT I HEAR	U.	TAIL AS BIG AS A KITE
22.	I WONDER AS I WANDER	V.	WHEN MARY BIRTHED JESUS
23.	O COME O COME EMANUEL	W.	AND RANSOM CAPTIVE ISRAEL
24.	DECK THE HALLS	X.	ANCIENT YULETIDE CAROL

25. WE THREE KINGS

Y. STAR OF WONDER STAR OF NIGHT

26. ONCE IN DAVID'S ROYAL CITY

Z. STOOD A LOWLY CATTLE SHED

MERRY CHRISTMAS (NOT RELIGIOUS)

1.	BLUE CHRISTMAS	A.	DECORATIONS OF RED
2.	FROSTY THE SNOWMAN	B.	CAME TO LIFE ONE DAY
3.	HAVE YOURSELF A MERRY	C.	WILL BE MILES AWAY
4.	HERE COMES SANTA CLAUS	D.	SANTA CLAUS LANE
5.	HOLLY JOLLY CHRISTMAS	E.	HAVE A CUP OF CHEER
6.	I SAW MOMMY KISSING SANTA	F.	DADDY HAD ONLY SEEN
7.	I'LL BE HOME FOR XMAS	G.	IF ONLY IN MY DREAMS
8.	IT'S BEGINNING TO LOOK	H.	IN THE FIVE AND TEN
9.	LET IT SNOW	I.	CORN FOR POPPING
10.	ROCKING AROUND	J.	CHRISTMAS PARTY HOP
11.	RUDOLPH THE RED NOSED	K.	DOWN IN HISTORY
12.	SANTA BABY	L.	HURRY DOWN THE CHIMNEY
13.	SANTA CLAUS IS COMING	M.	BETTER NOT POUT
14.	SILVER BELLS	N.	DRESSED IN HOLIDAY STYLE
15.	SLEIGH RIDE	O.	CALLING YOU HOO
16.	WHITE CHRISTMAS	P.	TREETOPS GLISTEN
17.	WINTER WONDERLAND	Q.	IN THE MEADOW
18.	ALL I WANT FOR XMAS	R.	IF I COULD ONLY WHISTLE
19.	THE CHIPMUNK SONG	S.	A HULA HOOP
20.	THE CHRISTMAS SONG	T.	YULETIDE CAROLS
21.	WE WISH YOU A MERRY CHRISTMAS	U.	GLAD TIDINGS WE BRING
22.	GRANDMA GOT RUN OVER	V.	NO SUCH THING AS SANTA
23.	THE GRINCH	W.	CUDDLY AS A CACTUS
24.	THE 12 DAYS OF CHRISTMAS	X.	LADIES DANCING
25.	O CHRISTMAS TREE	Y.	FAITHFUL ARE THY BRANCHES
26.	JINGLE BELL ROCK	Z.	DANCIN' AND PRANCIN'

U.S. VICE PRESIDENTS

1.	GEORGE WASHINGTON	A.	JOHN ADAMS
2.	ZACHARY TAYLOR	B.	MILLARD FILMORE
3.	JOHN F. KENNEDY	C.	LYNDON JOHNSON
4.	JOHN ADAMS	D.	THOMAS JEFFERSON
5.	RONALD REAGAN	E.	GEORGE H W BUSH
6.	ABE LINCOLN	F.	ANDREW JOHNSON
7.	JIMMY CARTER	G.	WALTER MONDALE
8.	WARREN G. HARDING	H.	CALVIN COOLIDGE
9.	HARRY TRUMAN	I.	ALBEN BARKLEY
10.	THOMAS JEFFERSON	J.	AARON BURR
11.	WM. MCKINLEY	K.	TEDDY ROOSEVELT
12.	LYNDON JOHNSON	L.	HUBERT HUMPHREY
13.	JAMES A GARFIELD	M.	CHESTER A. ARTHUR
14.	DWIGHT EISENHOWER	N.	RICHARD NIXON
15.	WM HENRY HARRISON	O.	JOHN TYLER
16.	FRANKLIN ROOSEVELT	P.	HARRY TRUMAN
17.	GEORGE W BUSH	Q.	RICHARD CHENEY
18.	GERALD FORD	R.	NELSON ROCKEFELLER
19.	ANDREW JOHNSON	S.	NONE
20.	RICHARD M NIXON	T.	SPIRO T AGNEW
21.	JAMES MADISON	U.	ELBRIDGE GERRY
22.	GEORGE H. W. BUSH	V.	J. DANFORTH QUALE
23.	JOHN QUINCY ADAMS	W.	JOHN C. CALHOUN
24.	GROVER CLEVELAND	X.	ADALI STEVENSON
25.	ULYSSES S. GRANT	Y.	HENRY WILSON
26.	WILLIAM CLINTON	Z.	ALBERT GORE, JR.

U.S. SENATORS THEN & NOW

1.	BARRY GOLDWATER	A.	ARIZONA
2.	DANIEL INOUYE	B.	HAWAII
3.	RICHARD NIXON	C.	CALIFORNIA
4.	EVERETT M. DIRKSEN	D.	ILLINOIS
5.	ORIN HATCH	E.	UTAH
6.	LYNDON B JOHNSON	F.	TEXAS
7.	CONNIE MACK	G.	FLORIDA
8.	BARBARA MIKULSKI	H.	MARYLAND
9.	FRED THOMPSON	I.	TENNESSEE
10.	JACOB JAVITS	J.	NEW YORK
11.	GARY HART	K.	COLORADO
12.	HUEY LONG	L.	LOUISIANA
13.	MARGARET CHASE SMITH	M.	MAINE
14.	JOHN F. KENNEDY	N.	MASSACHUSETTS
15.	JOE MCCARTHY	O.	WISCONSIN
16.	NANCY LANDON KASSEBAUM	P.	KANSAS
17.	STROM THURMOND	Q.	SOUTH CAROLINA
18.	CLAIBORNE PELL	R.	RHODE ISLAND
19.	SAM NUNN	S.	GEORGIA
20.	ALAN SIMPSON	T.	WYOMING
21.	BILL BRADLEY	U.	NEW JERSEY
22.	HATTIE WYATT CARAWAY	V.	ARKANSAS
23.	HUBERT H HUMPHREY	W.	MINNESOTA
24.	ROBERT BYRD	X.	WEST VIRGINIA
25.	JOHN GLENN	Y.	OHIO
26.	WILLIAM ROTH	Z.	DELAWARE

FAMOUS PAIRS

1.	LEWIS AND	A.	CLARK
2.	BURNS AND	B.	ALLEN
3.	ROGERS AND	C.	HAMMERSTEIN
4.	SACCO AND	D.	VANZETTI
5.	MARTIN AND	E.	LEWIS
6.	HORN AND	F.	HARDART
7.	SIMON AND	G.	GARFUNKEL
8.	BINNEY AND	H.	SMITH
9.	ABERCROMBIE AND	I.	FITCH
10.	ABBOTT AND	J.	COSTELLO
11.	LEA AND	K.	PERRINS
12.	FERRANTE AND	L.	TEICHER
13.	LEOPOLD AND	M.	LOEB
14.	SEARS AND	N.	ROEBUCK
15.	CURRIER AND	O.	IVES
16.	DUN AND	P.	BRADSTREET
17.	MARTINI AND	Q.	ROSSI
18.	GILBERT AND	R.	SULLIVAN
19.	BROOKS AND	S.	DUNN
20.	LERNER AND	T.	LOEWE
21.	JUSTERINI AND	U.	BROOKS
22.	SISKEL AND	V.	EBERT
23.	MASTERS AND	W.	JOHNSON
24.	MASON AND	X.	DIXON
25.	PENN AND	Y.	TELLER
26.	CRICK AND	Z.	WATSON

ALSO KNOWN AS

1. MARION MICHAEL MORRISON
2. NATHAN BIRNBAUM
3. SAMUEL LANGHORN CLEMENS
4. HENRY JOHN DEUTSCHENDORF JR.
5. CARYN JOHNSON
6. ARCHIBALD LEACH
7. FERDINAND L. ALCINDOR JR.
8. ALPHONSE D'ABRUZZO
9. ALLEN KONIGSBERG
10. ERNEST EVANS
11. THOMAS MAPOTHER 4TH.
12. ROBERT ZIMMERMAN
13. CASSIUS MARCELLUS CLAY JR.
14. CHERILYN SARKISIAN
15. BERNARD SCHWARTZ
16. FRANCES GUMM
17. GORDON SUMMER
18. LESLIE TOWNES HOPE
19. REGINALD DWIGHT
20. NORMA JEAN BAKER
21. BOBBY MOORE
22. CARLOS IRWIN ESTEVEZ
23. RICHARD STARKEY
24. KAROL WOJTYLA
25. VINCENT DAMON FURRIER
26. LESLIE LYNCH KING JR.

A. JOHN WAYNE
B. GEORGE BURNS
C. MARK TWAIN
D. JOHN DENVER
E. WHOOPI GOLDBERG
F. CARY GRANT
G. KAREEM ABDUL JABBAR
H. ALAN ALDA
I. WOODY ALLEN
J. CHUBBY CHECKER
K. TOM CRUISE
L. BOB DYLAN
M. MUHAMMAD ALI
N. CHER
O. TONY CURTIS
P. JUDY GARLAND
Q. STING
R. BOB HOPE
S. ELTON JOHN
T. MARILYN MONROE
U. AHMAD RASHAD
V. CHARLIE SHEEN
W. RINGO STARR
X. POPE JOHN PAUL II
Y. ALICE COOPER
Z. GERALD FORD

ODD JOB TITLES

1.	ARBITRAGEUR	A.	BUYS AND SELLS STOCKS
2.	BARRISTER	B.	COURTROOM ATTORNEY
3.	BEEFEATER	C.	TOWER OF LONDON GUARD
4.	CANINE PERAMBULATOR	D.	DOG WALKER
5.	CARTOGRAPHER	E.	MAP MAKER
6.	CHIROPODIST	F.	FOOT DOCTOR
7.	CONCIERGE	G.	HOTEL HEAD PORTER
8.	COOPER	H.	BARREL MAKER
9.	CROUPIER	I.	MANAGES A GAMING TABLE
10.	COSMETICIAN	J.	MAKE UP ARTIST
11.	GANDY DANCER	K.	RAIL ROAD CREW WORKER
12.	HABERDASHER	L.	MENS CLOTHIER
13.	KEY GRIP	M.	MOVES MOVIE SET EQUIPMENT
14.	LAPIDARY	N.	JEWELER
15.	LYRICIST	O.	PENS WORDS FOR SONGS
16.	MIXOLOGIST	P.	BARTENDER
17.	OCULIST	Q.	EYE DOCTOR
18.	ONCOLOGIST	R.	CANCER DOCTOR
19.	MILLINER	S.	MAKES WOMENS HATS
20.	PUGILIST	T.	BOXER
21.	ROUSTABOUT	U.	CIRCUS LABORER
22.	SOMMELIER	V.	WINE STEWARD
23.	STRUMPET	W.	LADY OF ILL REPUTE
24.	THESPIAN	X.	ACTOR
25.	VINTNER	Y.	WINEMAKER
26.	YEOMAN	Z.	U.S. NAVY CLERK

MATCH THE AUTHOR WITH THE WORK

1.	THE OLD MAN & THE SEA	A.	E. HEMMINGWAY
2.	DON QUIXOTE	B.	M. CERVANTES
3.	TREASURE ISLAND	C.	R. L. STEVENSON
4.	MOBY DICK	D.	H. MELVILLE
5.	SHOGUN	E.	J. CLAVELL
6.	JAYNE AYRE	F.	E. BRONTE
7.	ALICE IN WONDERLAND	G.	L. CARROLL
8.	THE GOOD EARTH	H.	P.S. BUCK
9.	HUNT FOR RED OCTOBER	I.	T. CLANCY
10.	JURRASIC PARK	J.	M. CRICHTON
11.	TALES OF THE SOUTH PACIFIC	K.	J. MICHENER
12.	THE WINDS OF WAR	L.	H. WOUK
13.	AROUND THE WORLD IN 80 DAYS	M.	J. VERNE
14.	ADVENTURES OF TOM SAWYER	N.	M. TWAIN
15.	PROFILES IN COURAGE	O.	J. F. KENNEDY
16.	CANTERBURY TALES	P.	G. CHAUCER
17.	HUNCHBACK OF NOTRE DAME	Q.	V. HUGO
18.	SILENT SPRING	R.	R. CARSON
19.	THE TIME MACHINE	S.	H. G. WELLS
20.	THE FALL/HOUSE OF USHER	T.	E. A. POE
21.	CATCH 22	U.	J. HELLER
22.	PRIDE & PREJUDICE	V.	J. AUSTEN
23.	CATCHER IN THE RYE	W.	J. D. SALINGER
24.	THE HOBBIT	X.	J.R.R. TOLKIEN
25.	ANIMAL FARM	Y.	G. ORWELL
26.	THE GRASS IS ALWAYS GREENER	Z.	E. BOMBECK

(OVER THE SEPTIC TANK)

COMPOSERS

1.	JOHN PHILLIP SOUSA	A.	THE STARS AND STRIPES FOREVER
2.	WOLFGANG MOZART	B.	EINE KLINE NACHTMUSIK
3.	AARON COPELAND	C.	HOEDOWN (FROM RODEO)
4.	LUDWIG VON BEETHOVEN	D.	ODE TO JOY (NINTH SYMPHONY)
5.	STEPHEN FOSTER	E.	MY OLD KENTUCKY HOME
6.	JOHANNES BRAHMS	F.	GERMAN REQUIEM
7.	HENRY MANCINI	G.	MOON RIVER
8.	J. S. BACH	H.	TOCCATA & FUGUE IN D.
9.	JOHN WILLIAMS	I.	THEME FROM MOVIE JAWS
10.	JOHANN STRAUSS II	J.	THE BLUE DANUBE
11.	LEROY ANDERSON	K.	SLEIGH RIDE
12.	ANTONIO VIVALDI	L.	THE FOUR SEASONS
13.	GEORGE GERSHWIN	M.	RHAPSODY IN BLUE
14.	CLAUDE DEBUSSY	N.	CLARE DE LUNE
15.	RICHARD WAGNER	O.	TRISTAN AND ISOLADE
16.	SCOTT JOPLIN	P.	THE MAPLE LEAF RAG
17.	PETER TCHAIKOWSKY	Q.	THE 1812 OVERTURE
18.	FRANZ LISZT	R.	HUNGARIAN RHAPSODY #12
19.	ALEXNADER BORODIN	S.	POLOVTSIAN DANCES
20.	EDVARD GRIEG	T.	PEER GYNT SUITES
21.	GEORGE BIZET	U.	THE TOREADOR'S SONG
22.	GUISEPPE VERDI	V.	LA TRAVIATA
23.	GIOACCHINO ROSSINI	W.	THE WILLIAM TELL OVERTURE
24.	MAURICE RAVEL	X.	BOLERO
25.	GIACOMO PUCCINI	Y.	NESSUM DORMA
26.	IRVING BERLIN	Z.	GOD BLESS AMERICA

A SAILORS VOCABULARY

1.	AFT	A.	TOWARDS THE REAR OF THE SHIP
2.	AMIDSHIPS	B.	IN THE MIDDLE OF THE SHIP
3.	BALLAST	C.	EXTRA WEIGHT FOR STABILITY
4.	BARGE	D.	FLAT BOTTOM CARGO CARRIER
5.	BEAM	E.	THE WIDTH OF THE SHIP
6.	BOATSWAIN	F.	BOSS OF ALL DECK HANDS
7.	BRIDGE	G.	WHERE THE CAPTAIN STEERS FROM
8.	BULKHEAD	H.	A WALL OF A SHIP
9.	CHANDLER	I.	ONE WHO SUPPLIES SHIPS
10.	COLLIER	J.	VESSEL TO TRANSPORT COAL
11.	DAVITS	K.	DEVICE A LIFEBOAT HANGS FROM
12.	DRAFT	L.	DEPTH OF A SHIP IN WATER
13.	FORCASTLE	M.	RAISED FRONT PART OF DECK
14.	GANGWAY	N.	PORTABLE WALKWAY TO GO ABOARD
15.	GUNWALE	O.	HIGHEST SIDE BOARD OF SHIP
16.	HAWSER	P.	A LARGE ROPE
17.	INTERMODAL	Q.	USING MORE THAN 1 TYPE OF TRANSPORT
18.	KNOT	R.	MEASUREMENT OF SPEED
19.	PANAMAX	S.	DESIGNED TO JUST FIT PANAMA CANAL
20.	PLIMSOL LINE	T.	DO NOT OVERLOAD LINE
21.	QUAY	U.	WHARF USED TO LOAD/UNLOAD
22.	SCRIMSHAW	V.	CARVINGS IN SHELL OR WHALEBONE
23.	SQUALL	W.	SUDDEN VIOLENT WIND OR STORM
24.	STARBOARD	X.	THE RIGHT SIDE OF THE SHIP
25.	TUG	Y.	POWERFUL SMALL BOAT
26.	WEIGH	Z.	TO HAUL UP (ESP THE ANCHOR)

A WORKING VOCABULARY

1.	BLACKSMITH	A.	ANVIL
2.	PILOT	B.	ALTIMETER
3.	SHIPWRIGHT	C.	FUTOCK
4.	CHEF	D.	TOQUE BLANCHE
5.	POET	E.	ONOMATOPOEIA
6.	SHEPHERD	F.	CROOK
7.	DRAFTSMAN	G.	PROTRACTOR
8.	BARTENDER	H.	JIGGER
9.	PRINTER	I.	EM
10.	MOHEL	J.	BRIS
11.	FLY FISHERMAN	K.	CREEL
12.	POTTER	L.	KILN
13.	SAILOR	M.	SCRIMSHAW
14.	HABBERDASHER	N.	CUMMERBUND
15.	TRUCKER	O.	JAKE BRAKE
16.	ROMAN CATHOLIC PRIEST	P.	MONSTRANCE
17.	POLITICIAN	Q.	GERRYMANDER
18.	FARMER	R.	HECTARE
19.	SOMMELIER	S.	JEROBOAM
20.	BUTCHER	T.	CLEAVER
21.	COWBOY	U.	LARIAT
22.	PC PROGRAMMER	V.	FORTRAN
23.	GUITAR PLAYER	W.	PLECTRUM
24.	SURGEON	X.	STENT
25.	PIANIST	Y.	METRONOME
26.	BRICKLAYER	Z.	HOD

THE FUNNY PAPERS

1.	DOONESBURY	A.	GARY TRUDEAU
2.	PEANUTS	B.	CHARLES SCHULTZ
3.	NANCY	C.	G & B GILCHRIST
4.	CATHY	D.	C. GUISEWITE
5.	GARFIELD	E.	JIM DAVIS
6.	FAMILY CIRCUS	F.	BIL KEANE
7.	DICK TRACY	G.	CHESTER GOULD
8.	HAGAR THE HORRIBLE	H.	CHRIS BROWNE
9.	BLONDIE	I.	CHIC YOUNG
10.	CALVIN & HOBBS	J.	BILL WATTERSON
11.	BEATTLE BAILEY	K.	MORT WALKER
12.	ALLEY OOP	L.	J & C BENDER
13.	THE LOCKHORNS	M.	HORST & REINER
14.	BRENDA STARR	N.	BRIGMAN & SCHMICH
15.	DENNIS THE MENACE	O.	HANK KETCHAM
16.	DILBERT	P.	SCOTT ADAMS
17.	ANDY CAPP	Q.	REG SMYTHE
18.	GASOLINE ALLEY	R.	FRANK KING
19.	HAZEL	S.	TED KEY
20.	THE FAR SIDE	T.	GARY LARSON
21.	WIZARD OF ID	U.	BRANT PARKER
22.	BC	V.	JOHNNY HART
23.	FRANK & ERNEST	W.	BOB THAVES
24.	MARMADUKE	X.	BRAD ANDERSON
25.	LUANN	Y.	GREG EVANS
26.	LIL ABNER	Z.	AL CAPP

GAMES PEOPLE PLAY

1.	MONOPOLY	A.	DO NOT PASS GO
2.	CHECKERS	B.	KING ME
3.	CANASTA	C.	SEVEN CARD MELD
4.	SCRABBLE	D.	TRIPLE WORD VALUE
5.	CLUE	E.	THE CONSERVATORY
6.	POKEMON	F.	PIKACHU
7.	CHESS	G.	EN PASSANT
8.	PINOCHLE	H.	JACK DIAMONDS / QUEEN SPADES
9.	RISK	I.	KAMCHATKA
10.	POKER	J.	ROYAL FLUSH
11.	20 QUESTIONS	K.	A BREAD BOX
12.	PARCHEESI	L.	HOME PATH
13.	CHUTES & LADDERS	M.	NAUGHTY DEEDS
14.	CHINESE CHECKERS	N.	MARBLES
15.	BACKGAMMON	O.	BLOT
16.	BOGGLE	P.	DOME
17.	CANDYLAND	Q.	GINGERBREAD HOUSE
18.	SCATTERGORIES	R.	20 SIDED DIE
19.	JENGA	S.	TOWER
20.	BACCARAT	T.	A NATURAL
21.	MAH JONGG	U.	WALL OF TILES
22.	BALDERDASH	V.	DASHER
23.	TRIVIAL PURSUIT	W.	PIE WEDGE
24.	DOMINOES	X.	MUGGINS
25.	LIFE	Y.	SPOUSE
26.	DUNGEONS AND DRAGONS	Z.	THE WIZARD

FOR REAL SPORTS

1.	GREEN BAY		A.	PACKERS
2.	DALLAS		B.	STARS
3.	KANSAS CITY		C.	ROYALS
4.	MIAMI		D.	HEAT
5.	JACKSONVILLE		E.	JAGUARS
6.	PHILADELPHIA		F.	KIXX
7.	BALTIMORE		G.	RAVENS
8.	BUFFALO		H.	BLIZZARD
9.	TENNESSEE		I.	TITANS
10.	ATLANTA		J.	THRASHERS
11.	HOUSTON		K.	COMETS
12.	MILWAUKEE		L.	WAVE
13.	TORNOTO		M.	RAPTORS
14.	PHOENIX		N.	COYOTES
15.	TAMPA BAY		O.	DEVIL RAYS
16.	OTTAWA		P.	REBEL
17.	SAN DIEGO		Q.	SPIRIT
18.	MINNESOTA		R.	WILD
19.	NASHVILLE		S.	PREDATORS
20.	CHARLOTTE		T.	STING
21.	WICHITA		U.	WINGS
22.	COLUMBUS		V.	LAND SHARKS
23.	WASHINGTON		W.	REDSKINS
24.	DETROIT		X.	SHOCK
25.	ALBANY		Y.	ATTACK
26.	CLEVELAND		Z.	COMETS

SPORTS STARS PAST

1.	BEN HOGAN	A.	GOLF (M)
2.	PEGGY FLEMING	B.	FIGURE SKATING (F)
3.	INGEMAR JOHANSSON	C.	BOXING
4.	RAFER JOHNSON	D.	DECATHALON
5.	STEVE CAUTHEN	E.	HORSE RACING (FLAT)
6.	JESSE OWENS	F.	TRACK & FIELD (M)
7.	MAUREEN CONNOLLY	G.	TENNIS (F)
8.	JACKIE STEWART	H.	GRAN PRIX RACING
9.	MARY DECKER	I.	TRACK & FIELD (F)
10.	ROGERS HORNSBY	J.	BASEBALL (NL)
11.	NADIA COMANNECI	K.	GYMNASTICS (F)
12.	PETE MARAVICH	L.	BASKETBALL
13.	SUSAN BUTCHER	M.	DOG SLED RACING
14.	DICK WEBER	N.	BOWLING
15.	JUDY RANKIN	O.	GOLF (F)
16.	JOE DALEY*	P.	ICE HOCKEY
17.	HARMON KILLEBREW	Q.	BASEBALL (AL)
18.	BRONKO NAGURSKI	R.	FOOTBALL
19.	STANLEY DANCER	S.	HORSE RACING (SULKY)
20.	GREG LUGANIS	T.	DIVING
21.	PICABO STREET	U.	SKIING (F)
22.	STAN SMITH	V.	TENNIS (M)
23.	PATTI WAGSTAFF	W.	AEROBATIC FLYING
24.	SCOTT HAMILTON	X.	FIGURE SKATING (M)
25.	MARK SPITZ	Y.	SWIMMING
26.	J.C. KILLY	Z.	SKIING (M)

* No relation to the author of this quiz

SPORTS VENUES

1.	ANAHEIM, CA	A.	ARROWHEAD POND
2.	BALTIMORE, MD	B.	CAMDEN YARDS
3.	BOSTON, MA	C.	FENWAY PARK
4.	CHICAGO, IL	D.	SOLDIER FIELD
5.	CLEVELAND, OH	E.	JACOBS FIELD
6.	DENVER, CO	F.	MC NICHOLS ARENA
7.	DETROIT, MI	G.	JOE LEWIS ARENA
8.	EDMONTON, AL	H.	SKY REACH CENTRE
9.	GREEN BAY, WI	I.	LAMBEAU FIELD
10.	INDIANAPOLIS	J.	MARKET SQUARE ARENA
11.	KANSAS CITY, MO	K.	ARROWHEAD STADIUM
12.	MONTREAL, PQ	L.	OLYMPIC STADIUM
13.	NYC (FLUSHING), NY	M.	SHEA STADIUM
14.	UNIONDALE, (LI), NY	N.	NASSAU COLISEUM
15.	KANATA, ON	O.	COREL CENTRE
16.	PHILADELPHIA, PA	P.	VETERANS STADIUM
17.	PITTSBURGH, PA	Q.	THREE RIVERS STADIUM
18.	PORTLAND, OR	R.	ROSE GARDEN
19.	ST. LOUIS, MO	S.	BUSCH STADIUM
20.	SAN DIEGO, CA	T.	QUALCOM STADIUM
21.	SAN FRANCISCO, CA	U.	3 COM STADIUM
22.	NASHVILLE, TN	V.	ADELPHIA STADIUM
23.	WASHINGTON, DC	W.	JACK KENT COOKE STADIUM

NOTE: Some are gone and some are now known by other names.

SPORTS TERMS

1.	BALK	A.	BASEBALL
2.	TURKEY	B.	BOWLING
3.	WICKET	C.	CRICKET
4.	SCRUM	D.	RUGBY
5.	FLETCH	E.	ARCHERY
6.	FRONTON	F.	JAI ALAI
7.	SILKS	G.	HORSE RACING
8.	BONSPIEL	H.	CURLING
9.	MASHIE	I.	GOLF
10.	CORNER KICK	J.	SOCCER
11.	GRIDIRON	K.	FOOTBALL
12.	PARRY	L.	FENCING
13.	LOVE	M.	TENNIS
14.	BOWSPRIT	N.	SAILING
15.	DOUBLE AXEL	O.	SKATING
16.	RACK	P.	POOL
17.	ZAMBONI	Q.	HOCKEY
18.	SINGLET	R.	WRESTLING
19.	RIMFIRE	S.	SHOOTING
20.	DEAD LIFT	T.	WEIGHTLIFTING
21.	SHOT CLOCK	U.	BASKETBALL
22.	CARABINER	V.	ROCK CLIMBING
23.	CREEL	W.	FISHING
24.	RESTRICTOR PLATE	X.	AUTO RACING
25.	SHUTTLECOCK	Y.	BADMINTON
26.	IMMELMANN	Z.	AEROBATICS

SPORTS NICKNAMES

1.	THE BABE	A.	GEORGE HERMAN RUTH
2.	THE GOLDEN JET	B.	BOBBY HULL
3.	SPLENDID SPLINTER	C.	TED WILLIAMS
4.	THE SHARK	D.	GREG NORMAN
5.	THE MAILMAN	E.	KARL MALONE
6.	THE BULL	F.	GREG LUZINSKI
7.	MODERN MR. ZERO	G.	TONY ESPOSITO
8.	MR. OCTOBER	H.	REGGIE JACKSON
9.	THE CYCLONE (CY)	I.	DENTON YOUNG
10.	THE HAMMER	J.	DAVE SHULTZ
11.	THE SNAKE	K.	KEN STABLER
12.	CHARLIE HUSTLE	L.	PETE ROSE
13.	THE BIG O	M.	OSCAR ROBERTSON
14.	BOOM BOOM	N.	BERNIE GEOFFRION
15.	THE REFRIGERATOR	O.	WILLIAM PERRY
16.	THE LOUISVILLE LIP	P.	MUHAMMAD ALI
17.	THE ROCKET	Q.	MAURICE RICHARD
18.	THE JUICE	R.	O.J. SIMPSON
19.	THE BIG UNIT	S.	RANDY JOHNSON
20.	THE ICEMAN	T.	GEORGE GERVIN
21.	THE GREAT ONE	U.	WAYNE GRETZKY
22.	THE HITMAN	V.	TOMMY HEARNS
23.	THE PEARL	W.	EARL MONROE
24.	THE GOLDEN BEAR	X.	JACK NICKLAUS
25.	THE SAY HEY KID	Y.	WILLIE MAYS
26.	YANKEE CLIPPER	Z.	JOE DIMAGGIO

BUILDINGS KNOWN BY NAME

1.	FALLINGWATER	A.	HOME BY FRANK LLOYD WRIGHT
2.	BLACK ROCK	B.	CBS HEADQUARTERS
3.	MONTICELLO	C.	HOME OF THOMAS JEFFERSON
4.	SCOTTY'S CASTLE	D.	MANSION IN DEATH VALLEY
5.	DRUMTHWACKET	E.	GOVERNOR'S MANSION, NJ
6.	THE HOUSE THAT RUTH BUILT	F.	YANKEE STADIUM
7.	THE HERMITAGE	G.	HOME OF ANDREW JACKSON
8.	THE BREAKERS	H.	THE VANDERBILT COTTAGE
9.	THE CASTLE	I.	SMITHSONIAN INST. ADMIN. OFFICES
10.	GRACIE MANSION	J.	MAYOR'S MANSION, NEW YORK CITY
11.	MOUNT VERNON	K.	ESTATE OF GEORGE WASHINGTON
12.	PICKFAIR	L.	RESIDENCE OF D. FAIRBANKS & MARY PICKFORD
13.	CHARTWELL	M.	ESTATE OF WINSTON CHURCHILL
14.	IOLANI PALACE	N.	ONLY ROYAL RESIDENCE IN THE U S
15.	TERRACE HILL	O.	GOVERNOR'S MANSION, IOWA
16.	ORCHARD HOUSE	P.	L. ALCOTT WROTE LITTLE WOMEN HERE
17.	FAIRLANE	Q.	ESTATE OF HENRY FORD
18.	U. S. NAVAL OBSERVATORY	R.	OFFICIAL RESIDENCE OF THE VICE PRESIDENT
19.	GRACELAND	S.	HOME OF ELVIS PRESLEY
20.	BEEHIVE HOUSE	T.	OFFICIAL RESIDENCE OF BRIGHAM YOUNG
21.	ARROWHEAD	U.	HERMAN MELVILLE FINISHED MOBY DICK HERE
22.	CASTLE GANDOLFO	V.	SUMMER HOME OF THE POPE
23.	HAUS WACHENFELD	W.	HITLER'S MOUNTAIN HOME
24.	THE OLD LADY OF THREADNEEDLE ST	X.	THE BANK OF ENGLAND

ATOMS AND MOLECULES

1.	AS	A.	ARSNIC
2.	AU	B.	GOLD
3.	C	C.	CARBON
4.	CA	D.	CALCIUM
5.	CU	E.	COPPER
6.	CAO	F.	LIME
7.	CH4	G.	METHANE
8.	CO2	H.	CARBON DIOXIDE
9.	Fe	I.	IRON
10.	Ar	J.	ARGON
11.	Ag	K.	SILVER
12.	Pb	L.	LEAD
13.	Hg	M.	MERCURY
14.	H	N.	HYDROGEN
15.	Na	O.	SODIUM
16.	Sn	P.	TIN
17.	I	Q.	IODINE
18.	W	R.	TUNGSTEN
19.	H2O	S.	WATER
20.	SiO2	T.	SAND
21.	NaCl	U.	SALT
22.	H2O2	V.	HYDROGEN PEROXIDE
23.	K	W.	POTASSIUM
24.	P	X.	PHOSPHORUS
25.	Ti	Y.	TITANIUM
26.	Cl	Z.	CHLORINE

MEASURING UP

1.	FATHOMS	A.	DEPTH OF WATER
2.	LUMENS	B.	FLOW OF LIGHT
3.	HECTARES	C.	LAND
4.	PECKS	D.	PRODUCE
5.	KNOTS	E.	SPEED ON OR IN WATER
6.	ANGSTROM UNITS	F.	LENGTH OF LIGHTWAVES
7.	SQUARE FEET	G.	HOUSING FLOOR PLAN
8.	REAMS	H.	QUANITITY OF PAPER
9.	B.T.U.S.	I.	HEAT
10.	EMS	J.	TYPE FONTS
11.	OHMS	K.	ELECTRICAL RESISTANCE
12.	FURLONGS	L.	HORSE RACE COURSES
13.	MACH NUMBERS	M.	SPEED IN THE AIR
14.	DECIBELS	N.	LOUDNESS OF SOUND
15.	CUBITS	O.	OLDEN LINEAR MEASURE
16.	HANDS	P.	HORSE HEIGHT
17.	ACRE FEET	Q.	WATER BEHIND A DAM
18.	PARSECS	R.	DISTANCE IN SPACE
19.	INCHES OF Hg	S.	AIR PRESSURE
20.	ON THE MOHS SCALE	T.	HARDNESS
21.	CARATS	U.	WEIGHT OF GEMS
22.	GILL	V.	BOOZE
23.	ON RICHTER SCALE	W.	EARTHQUAKES
24.	EPOCHS	X.	EARTH AGES
25.	BEAUFORT SCALE	Y.	WIND SPEED
26.	SCOVILLE UNITS	Z.	HEAT OF PEPPERS

PHOBIAS (REAL AND IMAGINED)

1.	ACOUSTICOPHOBIA	A.	NOISES
2.	ACROPHOBIA	B.	HEIGHTS
3.	AGORAHOBIA	C.	OPEN SPACES
4.	ANGLOPHOBIA	D.	THINGS ENGLISH
5.	ARACHNOPHOBIA	E.	SPIDERS
6.	AUTOPHOBIA	F.	ONESELF
7.	AVIOPHOBIA	G.	FLYING
8.	BIBLIOPHOBIA	H.	BOOKS
9.	CARCINOPHOBIA	I.	CANCER
10.	CLAUSTROPHOBIA	J.	CONFINED SPACES
11.	FRANCOPHOBIA	K.	THINKS FRENCH
12.	GYMNOPHOBIA	L.	NUDITY
13.	GYNOPHOBIA	M.	WOMEN
14.	HEDONOPHOBIA	N.	PLEASURE
15.	HELIOPHOBIA	O.	SUNLIGHT
16.	HEMOPHOBIA	P.	BLOOD
17.	HERPAPHOBIA	Q.	SNAKES
18.	HYDROPHOBIA	R.	WATER
19.	KLEPTOPHOBIA	S.	STEALING
20.	NECROPHOBIA	T.	THE DEAD
21.	PHOBOPHOBIA	U.	FEAR
22.	PYROPHOBIA	V.	FIRE
23.	SOMNIPHOBIA	W.	SLEEP
24.	THEOPHOBIA	X.	GOD
25.	TRISKAIDEKAPHOBIA	Y.	NUMBER 13
26.	XENOPHOBIA	Z.	FOREIGNERS

DEM BONES

1. KNEE CAPE
2. FUNNY BONE
3. THE EAR'S STIRRUP
4. SHINBONE
5. LONGEST NERVE
6. COLLARBONE
7. MAIN ARTERY FROM HEART
8. BREASTBONE
9. VEINS TO THE HEART
10. TAILBONE
11. TOES
12. WRIST BONES
13. LARGE FOREARM BONE
14. JAWBONE
15. THE LONGEST BONE

A. PATELLA
B. HUMERUS
C. STAPES
D. TIBIA
E. SCIATIC
F. CLAVICLE
G. AORTA
H. STERNUM
I. VENA CAVA
J. COCCYX
K. PHALANGES
L. CARPALS
M. ULNA
N. MANDIBLE
O. FEMUR

PILLS FOR EVERY PURPOSE

1.	LIPITOR	A.	HIGH CHOLESTEROL
2.	PRILOSEC	B.	ULCERS
3.	GLUCOPHAGE	C.	DIABETES
4.	AMOXICILLIN	D.	INFECTION
5.	CLARITIN	E.	SEASONAL ALLERGY
6.	PROZAC	F.	DEPRESSION
7.	IBUPROFEN	G.	PAIN, GENERAL
8.	ORTHO-NOVUM	H.	CONTRACEPTION
9.	ZYRTEC	I.	PERENNIAL ALLERGY
10.	VIAGRA	J.	IMPOTENCE
11.	DIAZEPAN	K.	EPILEPSY
12.	VALIUM	L.	ANXIETY
13.	NASONEX	M.	SINUS CONGESTION
14.	VASOTEC	N.	HYPERTENSION
15.	NITRO GLYCERIN	O.	ANGINA
16.	TAXOL	P.	BREAST CANCER
17.	ANBESOL	Q.	PAIN, DENTAL
18.	QUININE	R.	MALARIA
19.	RITALIN	S.	ATTENTION DEFICIT
20.	ALBUTEROL	T.	ASTHMA
21.	ROGAIN	U.	HAIR LOSS
22.	RISPERDAL	V.	PSYCHOSIS
23.	DIGOXIN	W.	CONGESTIVE HEART FAILURE
24.	PHAZYME	X.	FLATULENCE

THE SCHOOLS OF THE NCAA

1.	BRINGHAM YOUNG	A.	PROVO, UT
2.	BALL STATE.	B.	MUNCIE, IN
3.	BAYLOR U	C.	WACO, TX
4.	BUCKNELL U	D.	LEWISBURG, PA
5.	CANISIUS	E.	BUFFALO, NY
6.	COLGATE	F.	HAMILTON, NY
7.	CORNELL	G.	ITHACA, NY
8.	THE CITADEL	H.	CHARLESTON, SC
9.	DARTMOUTH	I.	HANOVER, NH
10.	DEPAUL U	J.	CHICAGO, IL
11.	DREXEL U	K.	PHILADELPHIA, PA
12.	DUKE U	L.	DURHAM, NC
13.	DUQUESNE U	M.	PITTSBURGH, PA
14.	FORDHAM U	N.	BRONX, NY
15.	GEORGETOWN	O.	WASHINGTON, DC
16.	GONZAGA	P.	SPOKANE, WA
17.	HOFSTRA U	Q.	HEMPSTEAD, NY
18.	LEHIGH U	R.	BETHELHEM, PA
19.	LOYOLA MARYMOUNT	S.	LOS ANGELES, CA
20.	OLD DOMINION	T.	NORFOLK, VA
21.	ORAL ROBERTS U	U.	TULSA, OK
22.	PEPPERDINE U	V.	MALIBU, CA
23.	US NAVAL ACADEMY	W.	ANNAPOLIS, MD
24.	US MILITARY ACADEMY	X.	WEST POINT, NY
25.	VANDERBILT U	Y.	NASHVILLE, TN
26.	WAKE FOREST	Z.	WINSTON-SALEM, NC

WORDS FROM A TO Z

1.	ANTHRACITE	A.	HARD COAL
2.	BOUYANT	B.	ABILITY TO FLOAT
3.	CHRISM	C.	SACRAMENTAL OIL
4.	DUCTILE	D.	NOT BRITTLE
5.	EGRESS	E.	AN EXIT
6.	FECUND	F.	FERTILE
7.	GUILE	G.	CUNNING
8.	HUMUS	H.	A TYPE OR PART OF SOIL
9.	INGENUE	I.	INNOCENT YOUNG GIRL
10.	JETSAM	J.	DISCHARGED FROM A SHIP
11.	KLEZMER	K.	A TYPE OF JEWISH MUSIC
12.	LANYARD	L.	A SHORT ROPE
13.	MUTATE	M.	TO CHANGE
14.	NAUTICAL	N.	HAVING TO DO WITH THE SEA
15.	OLIGARCHY	O.	RULE BY A FEW
16.	PICAYUNE	P.	PETTY/TRIVIAL
17.	QUAY	Q.	A DOCK OR WHARF
18.	RUE	R.	TO FEEL REMORSE
19.	SABATICAL	S.	PERIOD OF REST
20.	THORAX	T.	THE CHEST AREA
21.	UNGULATE	U.	A MAMMAL WITH HOOFS
22.	VERACITY	V.	HONESTY/TRUTHFULNESS
23.	WIMPLE	W.	WOMENS HEAD COVERING
24.	XENOPHOBIA	X.	HATRED OF FOREIGNERS
25.	YETI	Y.	ABOMINABLE SNOWMAN
26.	ZYDECO	Z.	CAJUN STYLE MUSIC

TV THEME SONGS

1.	ALL IN THE FAMILY	A.	LIKE H. HOOVER AGAIN
2.	ADDAMS FAMILY	B.	ALL TOGETHER OOKY
3.	BEVERLY HILLBILLIES	C.	A BUBBLIN CRUDE
4.	PATTY DUKE SHOW	D.	WHAT A CRAZY PAIR
5.	GILLIGAN'S ISLAND	E.	A THREE HOUR TOUR
6.	MR. ED	F.	OF COURSE, OF COURSE
7.	THE JEFFERSONS	G.	A PIECE OF THE PIE
8.	WKRP IN CINCINNATI	H.	PACKING & UNPACKING
9.	CHEERS	I.	SOMETIMES YOU WANT
10.	WONDER YEARS	J.	LEND ME YOUR EARS
11.	FRASIER	K.	SCRAMBLED EGGS
12.	FRESH PRINCE	L.	IN WEST PHILADELPHIA
13.	FRIENDS	M.	STUCK IN SECOND GEAR
14.	MARRIED WITH CHILDREN	N.	HORSE & CARRIAGE
15.	SUDDENLY, SUSAN	O.	THERE AIN'T MUCH HOPE
16.	BARETTA	P.	CAN'T DO THE TIME
17.	MOONLIGHTING	Q.	SOME FLY BY DAY
18.	WONDER WOMAN	R.	SATIN TIGHTS
19.	THE MUPPET SHOW	S.	LIGHT THE LIGHTS
20.	DAVY CROCKETT	T.	WHEN HE WAS ONLY 3
21.	ROY ROGERS	U.	KEEP SMILIN UNTIL THEN
22.	FAME	V.	I'M GONNA LEARN TO FLY
23.	MR. ROGERS	W.	COULD YOU BE MINE
24.	POPEYE	X.	I'M STRONG TO THE FINISH
25.	ANDY GRIFFITH SHOW	Y.	AT THE FISHIN HOLE
26.	BONANZA	Z.	HE'S GOTTA FIGHT WITH ME

I WAS FIRST

1. BREAK SOUND BARRIER (M)
2. PITCH A PERFECT GAME (1904)
3. CLIMB MOUNT EVEREST
4. FIRST MOVIE TARAZAN (DISP)
5. FLY ACROSS ATLANTIC SOLO
6. FIRST WOMAN IN SPACE
7. FIRST HEART TRANSPLANT
8. BREAK SOUND BARRIER (F)
9. PILOT FIRST FLIGHT (PLANE)
10. STEP ON THE MOON
11. BREAK 4 MINUTE MILE
12. DIE IN ELECTRIC CHAIR
13. EXCEED 600 MPH IN A CAR
14. SWIM ENGLISH CHANNEL (F)
15. FIRST WOMEN IN THE NHL
16. FIRST MAN IN SPACE
17. AMERICAN WOMAN MD
18. SOLD FROZEN FOOD
19. BUILT FIRST PC
20. BUILT 1ST STEAMBOAT
21. 1ST 'INSTANT' CAMERA
22. 1ST USEFUL ELEVATOR
23. ICE RESURFACER
24. PHONOGRAPH MACHINE
25. 1ST AMERICAN SAINT
26. FIRST CHILD BORN IN AMERICA
    OF EUROPEAN PARENTS

A. CHUCK YEAGER
B. MIKE MORRISON
C. EDMUND HILLARY
D. ELMO LINCOLN
E. CHARLES LINDBURGH
F. VALENTINA TERESHKOVA
G. CHRISTIAAN BARNHARD
H. JACQUELINE COCHRAN
I. ORVILLE WRIGHT
J. NEIL ARMSTRONG
K. ROGER BANNISTER
L. WILLIAM KEMMLER
M. CRAIG BREEDLOVE
N. GERTRUDE EDERLY
O. MANON RHEAUME
P. YURI GAGARIN
Q. ELIZABETH BLACKWELL
R. CLARENCE BIRDSEYE
S. STEVEN JOBS
T. ROBERT FULTON
U. EDWIN LAND
V. ELISHA OTIS
W. FRANK ZAMBONI
X. THOMAS EDISON
Y. ELIZABETH A SETON

Z. VIRGINIA DARE

WEIRD TOOLS

1.	BRACE AND BIT	A.	A HAND DRILL
2.	ENTERENCHING TOOL	B.	A SOLDIERS SHOVEL
3.	CLAVICLE BOARD	C.	KEY HOLDER
4.	FIFTH WHEEL	D.	CONNECTS TRACTOR & TRAILER
5.	HEMOSTAT	E.	SURGICAL CLAMP
6.	HAWSER	F.	LARGE ROPE USED ON SHIPS
7.	CHURCH KEY	G.	BOTTLE OPENER
8.	ABACUS	H.	ORIENTAL COUNTING DEVICE
9.	BOLA	I.	GAUCHOS THROWING WEAPON
10.	EPEE	J.	FENCING SWORD
11.	TRANSIT	K.	SURVEYORS TELESCOPE
12.	AUTOCLAVE	L.	STERLIZING MACHINE
13.	PLECTRUM	M.	GUITAR PICK
14.	OBOE	N.	DOUBLE REED HORN
15.	VALISE	O.	A TYPE OF SUITCASE
16.	PESTLE	P.	A GRINDING (CRUSHING) TOOL
17.	SPANNER	Q.	FIREMANS HOSE WRENCH
18.	ZIP DRIVE	R.	COMPUTER STORAGE DEVICE
19.	GIMBALED CHRONOMETER	S.	SHIPS PRECISE NAVIGATION CLOCK
20.	PETRI DISH	T.	WHERE A LAB GROWS MICROOGANISMS
21.	BATON	U.	A MAESTRO'S STICK
22.	ARTIFICAL HORIZON	V.	A PILOTS ATTITUDE INDICATOR
23.	LINTEL	W.	CROSSMEMBER OVER A DOOR
24.	DAVIT	X.	LIFE BOAT LOWERING DEVICE
25.	ODOMETER	Y.	MEASURES MILES DRIVEN
26.	SHILLELAGH	Z.	AN IRISHMAN'S CLUB

WHERE AM I?

1.	AREA 51	A.	NEVADA
2.	KHYBER PASS	B.	AFGHANISTAN
3.	SEA OF TRANQUILLITY	C.	THE MOON
4.	THE GRAND CANYON	D.	ARIZONA
5.	LOCH NESS	E.	SCOTLAND
6.	NAPA VALLEY	F.	CALIFORNIA
7.	GOLAN HEIGHTS	G.	ISRAEL
8.	BAY OF PIGS	H.	CUBA
9.	BLACK FOREST	I.	GERMANY
10.	MEKONG DELTA	J.	VIETNAM
11.	LAKE OKEECHOBEE	K.	FLORIDA
12.	THE ALHAMBRA	L.	SPAIN
13.	THE PAMPAS	M.	ARGENTINA
14.	DIAMOND HEAD	N.	HAWAII
15.	THE GINZA	O.	JAPAN
16.	THE NILE DELTA	P.	EGYPT
17.	GREAT SALT LAKE	Q.	UTAH
18.	THE GRAND BANKS	R.	CANADA
19.	NORTH ISLAND	S.	NEW ZEALAND
20.	THE GREAT FJORDS	T.	NORWAY
21.	KOWLOON	U.	HONG KONG
22.	CORREGIDOR	V.	PHILIPPINES
23.	BIG BEN	W.	ENGLAND
24.	TAJ MAHAL	X.	INDIA
25.	PUGET SUOND	Y.	WASHINGTON
26.	CHICHEN ITZA	Z.	MEXICO

MIDDLE NAMES

1.	ALVA	A.	THOMAS EDISON
2.	BIRCHARD	B.	RUTHERFORD HAYES
3.	CASH	C.	JAMES PENNEY
4.	DELANO	D.	FRANKLIN ROOSEVELT
5.	EARL	E.	JAMES (JIMMY) CARTER
6.	FITZGERALD	F.	JOHN KENNEDY
7.	GAMALIEL	G.	WARREN HARDING
8.	HORATIO	H.	HUBERT HUMPHREY
9.	ILLICH	I.	VLADIMIR LENIN
10.	JAMES	J.	JOHN AUDUBON
11.	KING	K.	NAT COLE
12.	LAW	L.	BERNARD MONTGOMERY
13.	MILHOUS	M.	RICHARD NIXON
14.	NANCE	N.	JOHN GARNER
15.	ORVILLE	O.	WILLIAM DOUGLAS
16.	PIERPONT	P.	JOHN MORGAN
17.	QUINCY	Q.	JOHN ADAMAS
18.	RICE	R.	EDGAR BURROUGHS
19.	SNAVLEY	S.	MILTON HERSHEY
20.	TECUMSHA	T.	WILLIAM SHERMAN
21.	VICTOR	V.	EUGENE DEBS
22.	WENDELL	W.	OLIVER HOLMES
23.	XAVIER	X.	FRANK FELLER

ADS WE ALL KNOW

1. YOU DESERVE A BREAK TODAY
2. _____ TASTES GOOD LIKE A _____ SHOULD.
3. THINGS GO BETTER WITH _____
4. ONLY _____ _____ KNOWS FOR SURE
5. SOMETHING SPECIAL IN THE _____.

6. I'D WALK A MILE FOR A _____.
7. TAKES A LICKING & KEEPS ON TICKING.
8. HOME OF THE WHOPPER
9. MADE FROM THE BEST STUFF ON EARTH
10. WE TRY HARDER
11. I'D RATHER FIGHT THAN SWITCH.
12. SEE THE U.S.A. IN YOUR
13. TIME WELL SPENT
14. LET _____ TAKE YOU HOME
15. YOUR IN GOOD HANDS WITH _____

16. 99.44/100 PURE
17. WE NEVER SLEEP.

18. THE COMPANY YOU KEEP
19. DON'T LEAVE HOME WITHOUT IT
20. WHEN IT RAINS, IT POURS
21. A LITTLE DAB WILL DO YA
22. WE BRING GOOD THINGS TO LIFE
23. NOBODY DOESN'T LIKE _____
24. GOOD TO THE LAST DROP
25. ITS BETTER IN THE
26. I CAN'T BELIEVE I ATE THE WHOLE THING

A. MC DONALDS
B. WINSTON
C. COKE
D. LADY CLAIROL
E. AMERICAN AIRLINES
F. CAMEL
G. TIMEX
H. BURGER KING
I. SNAPPLE
J. AVIS
K. TARRYTON
L. CHEVROLET
M. A & E CHANNEL
N. ATLAS (VAN LINES)
O. ALLSTATE INSURANCE
P. IVORY SOAP
Q. PINKERTOWN DECTECTIVES
R. NEW YORK LIFE
S. AMERICAN EXPRESS
T. MORTON SALT
U. BRYLCREME
V. G. E.
W. SARA LEE
X. MAXWELL HOUSE
Y. BAHAMAS.
Z. ALKA SELTZER

MORE ADS

1.	MMM GOOD	A.	CAMPBELL SOUP
2.	HAVE IT YOUR WAY	B.	BURGER KING
3.	YOU'RE GETTIN A—DUDE	C.	DELL (COMPUTER)
4.	SOMETIMES YOU FEEL LIKE A NUT	D.	ALMOND JOY
5.	SOMETIMES YOU DON'T	E.	MOUNDS
6.	BREAKFAST OF CHAMPIONS	F.	WHEATIES
7.	NO MORE TEARS	G.	J & J BABY SHAMPOO
8.	I'M WORTH IT	H.	PREFERNCE BY L'OREAL
9.	DIAMONDS ARE FOREVER	I.	DE BEERS
10.	I LOVE	J.	NEW YORK
11.	_____ SEEDS GROW	K.	BURPEE
12.	GOT _____	L.	MILK
13.	I WISH I WERE AN	M.	OSCAR MEYER WIENER
14.	WE ANSWER TO A HIGHER AUTHORITY	N.	HEBREW NAT'L HOT DOGS
15.	FINGER LICKIN GOOD	O.	KFC
16.	HEAD FOR THE MOUNTAINS	P.	BUSCH BEER
17.	HEAD FOR THE BORDER	Q.	TACO BELL
18.	DON'T SQUEEZE THE	R.	CHARMIN
19.	JUST DO IT	S.	NIKE
20.	MELTS IN YOUR MOUTH	T.	M & M'S
21.	HOW DO YOU SPELL RELIEF	U.	ROLAIDS
22.	IT'S SHOT FROM GUNS	V.	QUAKER PUFFED WHEAT
23.	PROMISE HER ANYTHING	W.	ARPEGE PERFUME
24.	EVERYWHERE YOU WANT TO BE	X.	VISA CARD
25.	IT'S THE REAL THING	Y.	COKE
26.	TAKE IT OFF TAKE IT ALL OFF	Z.	NOXEMA

PRE PRESIDENTIAL JOBS

1.	PEANUT FARMER	A.	JIMMY CARTER
2.	TAILOR	B.	ANDREW JOHNSON
3.	MINING ENGINEER	C.	HERBERT HOOVER
4.	COLLEGE PRESIDENT	D.	WOODROW WILSON
5.	CHIEF JUSTICE OF THE U. S. (POST PRES.)	E.	W. H. TAFT
6.	LABOR UNION LEADER	F.	RONALD REAGAN
7.	PRINTER (NEWSPAPER OWNER)	G.	WARREN G. HARDING
8.	HABERDASHER	H.	HARRY TRUMAN
9.	LEATHER MAKER	I.	U. S. GRANT
10.	ASST. FOOTBALL COACH	J.	GERALD FORD
11.	POSTMASTER	K.	ABE LINCOLN
12.	CIA DIRECTOR	L.	GEORGE BUSH
13.	LAND SURVEYOR	M.	GEORGE WASHINGTON
14.	ASST. SECRETARY OF THE NAVY	N.	F. D. ROOSEVELT
15.	MINISTER TO RUSSIA (& A BACHELOR)	O.	JAMES BUCHANAN
16.	SMALL COMBAT BOAT CAPTAIN	P.	J. F. KENNEDY
17.	CATTLE RANCHER	Q.	T. ROOSEVELT
18.	FIVE STAR GENERAL	R.	D. D. EISENHOWER
19.	TEACHER (PUBLIC SPEAKING)	S.	L. B. JOHNSON
20.	CANAL BOATMAN (NY)	T.	JAMES A. GARFIELD
21.	SON OF A U.S. PRESIDENT	U.	JOHN QUINCY ADAMS
22.	U. S. PRESIDENT (NON CONSECUTIVE)	V.	GROVER CLEVELAND
23.	FARMER, INVENTOR, SCIENTIST, LINGUIST, ARCHITECT, PHILOSOPHER ETC, ETC, ETC.	W.	THOMAS JEFFERSON